W9-COI-258

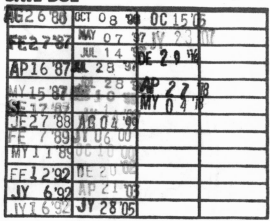

THE ARCTIC PATROL MYSTERY

PRIVATE investigator Fenton Hardy enlists the aid of his teen-age detective sons in a search for a missing man being sought by an insurance company. All leads to the sailor's whereabouts have petered out and the boys fly to Iceland, the man's native land, hoping to find a new clue.

From the moment Frank and Joe arrive in Reykjavik, the capital city of Iceland, they are in constant danger. They are shadowed by a mysterious blond man who is later responsible for the crash landing of their chartered plane on a vast glacier. Stranded in a fierce blizzard, the detective brothers narrowly escape death. Other perils confront them when their friends Chet Morton and Biff Hooper vanish under alarming circumstances.

In the spine-chilling pursuit that follows, Frank and Joe uncover a diabolical espionage plot that threatens the life of a U.S. astronaut and NASA's moon project.

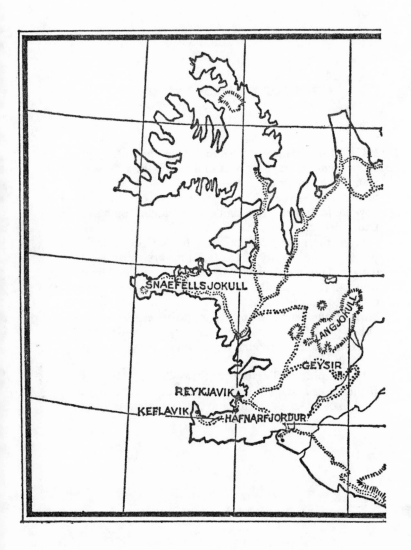

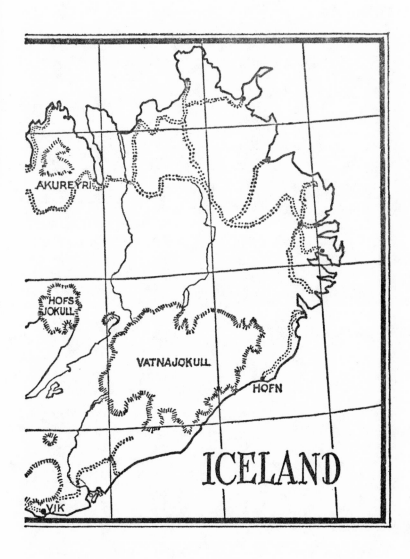

Hardy Boys Mystery Stories

THE
ARCTIC PATROL
MYSTERY

BY

FRANKLIN W. DIXON

GROSSET & DUNLAP
Publishers • New York

CONTENTS

CHAPTER I

Icelandic Secret

"How would you boys like to fly to Iceland?"
Mr. Hardy asked his sons.

Frank and Joe, seated in their father's study
on the second floor of the Hardy home in Bayport, looked stunned.

"Iceland? Up near the Arctic Circle?" asked
blond-haired, seventeen-year-old Joe.

Frank, dark-haired and a year older, had the
same incredulous look as his brother, but he realized that his famous detective father was not jok-
ing. "Of course, Dad! What's the pitch? Another
mystery?"

Fenton Hardy rocked slightly in his high-
backed swivel chair. "I would call it a mild mystery compared with some others you've handled.
But it could develop into the most dangerous
one yet, provided . . ." Frowning, he paused for
a moment.

Joe queried excitedly, "Provided what, Dad?"

"That depends on another assignment I'm not at liberty to reveal. It's top secret—for the moment at least. Your job is to find a man named Rex Hallbjornsson. An insurance company wants to pay him fifty thousand dollars."

Frank smiled. "That's not hard to take. Who left him that tidy little fortune?"

"A person whose life he saved at sea."

"Then this Hallb—what's his name—is a sailor?" Joe asked.

"Right. Probably one reason why Hallbjornsson hasn't been found. And I have a hunch his long Scandinavian name might have something to do with it, too."

Mr. Hardy quickly outlined the important facts. The missing man's last known address was a London steamship company. That was before his ship was sunk by a drifting mine off the coast of France. European detectives tracked him to a family on the coast of Brittany, but Hallbjornsson had long since gone from there. He did leave a clue—a scrap of paper which bore the word 'Island.'

"Island is the Icelandic word for Iceland," Mr. Hardy explained. "Hallbjornsson would be in his sixties by now. My guess is that he returned to his native land. Your mission—track him down. There's a direct flight from New York to Reykjavik, the capital of Iceland."

"What about Chet?" Joe asked. "Can he come with us?"

Chet Morton was the Hardys' best friend. He was a stout boy, great as a lineman on the Bayport High football team, but less than enthusiastic as a sleuth. Chet would side-step danger, if possible. However, when the chips were down, he always proved to be a true pal. He was fond of food and hobbies, the latter changing as often as the weather.

Mr. Hardy pondered the question about Chet in silence for a few moments. "Yes," he said finally, "Chet might be of assistance as well as good company. But you must warn him to be silent. Premature disclosure of our plans could prove disastrous."

Frank and Joe made careful note of their father's warning, because Fenton Hardy was an expert in detective work and security. He had been a crack member of the New York Police Department, and his superiors hated to lose him when he left to start his own agency. Now he was world-famous and his sons were following in his footsteps.

Their first case, known as *The Tower Treasure,* had whetted the boys' appetite for mysteries, and they had solved one after another, their latest being *Mystery of the Whale Tattoo.*

"Great, Dad!" Frank said, jumping to his feet.

"With spring vacation coming up we won't miss any time at school!"

"Are your passports up to date?" his father asked.

"Sure, we always keep them that way."

A telephone call brought Chet Morton and his old jalopy backfiring to a halt in front of the Hardy home on Elm Street. Chet lived on a farm several miles out of town. He had a sister, Iola, who was Joe's girl friend.

Frank's special date was Callie Shaw. But girls were far from the minds of the young detectives as they ran out to greet their friend.

Chet hopped out of the car, his round face beaming. "Hi, fellows. Another mystery? By the way, how's your Aunt Gertrude fixed for pie?"

"Come in. We'll find out."

Laura Hardy, the boys' mother, had gone marketing, leaving Aunt Gertrude in sole charge of the kitchen. Miss Hardy, their father's sister, was tall, spare, and decisive.

She often looked askance at the mysteries in which her nephews became involved. Nonetheless, Frank and Joe were very special to her as was Chet Morton, chief connoisseur of her excellent culinary abilities.

"Well! You sound like a bunch of elephants tramping in here!" Aunt Gertrude said.

"Chet's hungry again," Frank declared with a wink.

"What else?" Joe joked. "That's a permanent condition with him."

"Aw, cut it out, fellows," said Chet, pulling out a kitchen chair and sliding his ample frame into it. "What's your latest in pies, Aunt Gertrude?"

Miss Hardy pursed her lips in a mock look of annoyance, yet she was secretly pleased with her reputation as a baker.

"Rhubarb pie, Chester. It's chilling in the refrigerator."

A sly smile spread over Chet Morton's face. He leaned forward, elbows on the table. "My favorite! You must have known I was coming!"

"Cut out the baloney, Chet," said Joe. "You'd eat anything."

Chet's hurt look vanished when a large wedge of pie was placed before him, along with a tall glass of milk.

"Thank you, thank you," he said as Aunt Gertrude left to take care of other household chores. Then he turned to his friends. "Now what's this latest proposition?"

"We're going to Iceland," Frank said seriously, "and would like to take you with us."

Chet grinned broadly. "Good thought!"

"But you must keep this absolutely mum," Joe warned. "Not a word of it to anyone."

"You can trust me to be quiet," Chet stated between mouthfuls.

"And we mean *quiet!*" Frank added emphatically.

"Okay, I'm with you." Chet savored a long swig of milk. "And what are we going to do there?"

Briefly the Hardys told of their mission, and Chet seemed delighted with the idea. "Finding somebody doesn't seem too dangerous," he said. "Besides, I'd like to see some real Eskimos."

As he finished speaking, Chet banged the side of his hand on the kitchen table, making the pie plate jump.

"What are you trying to do?" Joe demanded.

"Just practicing my karate chop."

"Your latest hobby?" Frank asked.

"Sure. The art of self-defense. Got to get the old hands toughened up. Never can tell when you need it."

"You're a nut," Joe said, grinning, as the boys stood up and walked to the front door.

"Thanks for the pie," Chet said to Gertrude Hardy whom they met in the hall. "It'll give me lots of strength for our next case."

"Quiet!" Joe said. "You're spilling the beans already."

Aunt Gertrude sniffed, as if scenting a danger, and her eyebrows raised above the rim of her glasses. "Another case?" she asked, looking from Frank to Joe. "What is it?"

"Something simple," Frank assured her. "An easy investigation. Don't worry."

"Just practicing my karate chop," Chet said

"Humph! I worry all the time about you."

"We're only going to Iceland," said Joe.

"Iceland?" Aunt Gertrude made a face as if the entire country were run by wild, long-haired Vikings. "You'll freeze to death up there, if you're not eaten by a polar bear!"

"Or lost on the stormy seas," Joe added.

"Don't get smart, young man," his aunt replied, and marched into the kitchen, where she put the remaining pie and the milk back into the refrigerator.

Frank remembered studying about Iceland in school and knew that the weather should be mild in April, although there were occasional storms in the area at that time of year. "Bring some heavy clothes just in case," he told his friend.

"How about skis and snowshoes?"

"Forget it, Chet. I didn't say the North Pole!"

"What about the rest of the gang? Shall I tell them?" asked Chet.

Frank hesitated. "Dad cautioned us not to say anything to anybody."

"Well, Tony and Biff will know the next day that we're gone," Joe put in. "Suppose we tell them we're going away on a secret mission without saying where."

"Okay," Frank agreed. "Maybe we can have a get-together before we leave."

"Good idea." Chet said good-by and chugged off. He made a stop at the Bayport Hardware

Store for some farm supplies before heading back home.

As Chet hefted a bale of peat moss to his shoulder and carried it to his jalopy, he nearly bumped into Fred Marney, who broadcast the news on the Bayport TV channel. Marney was well acquainted with the exploits of the Hardys and their friends.

"Hi, Chet. Getting the garden ready?" he greeted the boy.

"Not me. This is for my mother's roses. No time for gardening."

"What? With spring vacation coming up?"

"Oh, I'll be busy," said Chet and moved toward the car.

"Busy with what?" Marney persisted. "Another Hardy boys' case?"

Chet tossed the bale to the back of the car and turned to frown at the broadcaster.

"So I hit the nail on the head, eh?" the newsman persisted.

"I didn't say *anything!*" Chet said, sliding behind the wheel. "The trip to Iceland is nobody's business except—"

Chet could have bitten off his tongue as Marney smirked and turned away. He had broken his promise! What would the Hardys say now? Well, maybe it was of so little importance that Fred Marney would forget it.

That evening, just before the TV newscast,

Chet got a phone call from Tony Prito. "Listen, Chet, big doings at our place tonight. My mother's giving a pizza feast. The whole bunch will be here. I told Iola already. Come with your appetite."

"Then you know about the trip?" Chet asked.

"Biff and I do, but that's all. Frank and Joe want to keep it a secret."

"Yeah, I know about that," Chet said limply. "I'll be there, but I don't know about my appetite."

Tony Prito laughed as he hung up, and Chet tuned in the evening report. His eyes were glued to the TV screen. National news came first, then other reports of statewide importance, and finally an item about the Bayport city council. Chet breathed a sigh of relief. His secret had not been violated!

In the Hardy home Frank, Joe, and Mr. Hardy were watching the same program while the boys' mother and Aunt Gertrude were preparing supper. After the council report Fred Marney smiled at his viewers and said, "And now a little juicy tidbit for fans of the famous Hardy boys." Frank and Joe froze and Mr. Hardy frowned deeply.

The reporter went on, "This time it's a trip to Iceland for Frank and Joe and, of course, their pal Chet Morton, too. Since this is not a junket for fun in the sun, we wonder what the detectives are up to now."

"Holy crow!" Joe exclaimed and flicked off the set. "How did he find out about that?"

"I'm afraid this means trouble," Mr. Hardy said, thumping a fist into the palm of his hand. "Well, what's done is done!"

"Do you suppose it was Chet?" asked Frank.

The answer came with the ringing of the telephone. Joe grabbed it. The voice on the other end was so low that he could hardly hear it. "What? . . . Oh, it's you, Chet. . . . Yes, we heard." There was a long silence while Chet explained.

Then Joe went on, "No, I don't think it'll wash out the trip, but Dad's very much upset. See you later."

Joe told the others what had happened, which was not of much comfort to his father. After supper Mr. Hardy announced that he was leaving for an important secret meeting.

Frank and Joe showered and dressed for the party in the Pritos' rumpus room. Chet was bringing his sister Iola, and Frank was to pick up Callie Shaw at her home. Just as the boys started out to their car, they heard the phone ring.

Aunt Gertrude answered. After listening for a few moments, she said, "You shouldn't play pranks like this, Callie Shaw! What is it you—?" Then she turned to the boys with an astonished expression on her face. "Goodness, she hung up on me!"

"That couldn't have been Callie," Frank said. "She wouldn't do a thing like that!"

"What did the caller say?" Joe asked.

"She claimed it was the White House calling Fenton Hardy."

The boys climbed into their convertible, uneasy about the strange call. Had it been a joke?

"We'd better not mention this to anyone," Frank said. Joe agreed.

A few minutes later they pulled up at the Shaws' house, and Frank hurried to pick up his pretty blond date.

When they arrived at Tony Prito's place, Frank parked in front of the house, and the three entered. Chet and his vivacious, dark-haired sister were already there. They all trooped down to the basement, where brawny Biff Hooper and good-looking Tony were playing a game of Ping-Pong.

Their dates were shouting encouragement to the two, when Tony sent a sizzling backhand shot which nicked the end of the table.

"You win!" Biff said and put down his paddle. "Hi, Frank, Joe! The news is all over town!"

When Frank remained silent, Tony said, "Hey, you guys, where's your bounce tonight?"

"The news shouldn't have gotten out," Joe explained. "Well, let's forget about the whole thing and have some fun."

The boys grabbed billiard cues and went to the large table which occupied one end of the basement. Callie, meanwhile, put on some dance records, and as the evening progressed, the fun increased until Mrs. Prito appeared carrying a large tray of red-hot pizza.

Frank touched Callie's arm. "I'd like to get out for a little fresh air before we tackle the goodies."

"Me, too," Callie replied. "It's stuffy in here."

The couple stepped out into the star-studded evening. As they walked toward the front of the house, Frank noticed a car parked five feet from the curb, almost directly behind his convertible. All its doors were open.

Three men approached Frank as he walked forward. Callie lingered behind. When the man in the lead had almost reached Frank, he suddenly commanded, "Come with us!"

Callie stifled a scream and ran back into the house!

CHAPTER II

Thug for Hire

FRANK sized up the situation in a split second. The doors of the car stood open, and its motor was running. All prepared, Frank thought, to receive the kidnap victim.

The young detective dodged the man in front of him, raced through the clutching hands of the other two, and dived into the car. In a twinkling he had it in gear and floored the accelerator.

Whoosh! Tires screeched as the car bolted ahead. It zigzagged wildly, its doors flying, until Frank gained control and spun around the corner. Now to get back to the thugs as quickly as possible!

Frank circled the block and returned to the Prito house, where everyone was standing on the front lawn.

Only one thug was in evidence, flat on his back, with Tony kneeling on his chest. Moments later two police cars, blinkers flashing, raced up. Bayport's Chief Collig jumped out, followed by his driver. Patrolman Riley leaped from the other car.

"What's going on?" Collig asked crisply. He was a portly, middle-aged man, a close confidant of the Hardys.

"A kidnap attempt," Frank said.

"Here's the one we caught!" Tony said. "The other two got away." He pulled the man to his feet. He was thin and of medium height with sunken cheeks and bulging eyes. Tony's hand twisted the thug's shirt front, until the man winced.

"Who are you?" Tony demanded.

"And your pals?" Joe added.

But the captive would not talk.

"We probably have a file on him," Chief Collig said. He handcuffed the prisoner and turned him over to Riley. Then he went to his car and radioed headquarters. Returning, the police chief stated, "We'll search for the other two men, don't worry."

"Thanks," Frank said, and the young people went back to their party.

After refreshments, Frank and Joe dropped Callie off, then drove home. Mr. Hardy was not back yet, and Frank told their mother what had happened.

He had just finished when the lights of the detective's car swept the front windows as it pulled into the driveway. Mr. Hardy entered through the back door, looking serious.

When he heard about the kidnapping attempt, he shook his head. "I'm sorry I got you involved in this whole nasty business."

"Don't worry, Dad," Joe said. "We can take care of ourselves."

Mr. Hardy seemed lost in thought for a moment, then asked, "Anyone telephone while I was gone?"

"No, dear," his wife replied, but added quickly, "Oh, yes, someone did call. Gertrude thought it was a joke."

Mr. Hardy glanced at her in alarm. "Where was the call from?"

"The White House—at least that's what the girl said."

The detective gave a low whistle and shook his head again.

"What's wrong, Dad?" Frank asked sympathetically. He had never seen his father so dejected.

The detective managed a smile and looked at his sons. "I can't tell you now," he said. "Later, perhaps." He gave each boy a pat on the back, then climbed the stairs to his study.

Frank and Joe went to bed, wondering what it was all about. A little later they heard their father go to his bedroom and then make a telephone call on the upstairs hall extension. He spoke in low tones and they could not hear what he was saying.

In the middle of the night, both boys were

awakened by Mr. Hardy's footsteps going downstairs. Joe leaped up and opened the door a crack. He heard his father greet two men in whispered tones. Then he led them upstairs to his study.

"Holy crow!" Frank whispered. "This is regular cloak-and-dagger stuff, Joe!"

"You can say that again!"

They returned to bed and slept fitfully until morning. At breakfast no mention was made of the mysterious callers.

Finally Mr. Hardy said, "Boys, I'm going on a special mission to Texas. There's something I want to give you to take to Iceland."

Frank and Joe followed him to his study. He unlocked one of the drawers of his desk and pulled out what looked like a small transistor radio.

"What's that?" Joe asked.

"It's the latest in decoders," Mr. Hardy replied, "and it works on the decibel principle."

He explained that the high peaks of sound in any conversation were the keys to the code. "Once you have established these," he said, "the message can be decoded by using this special book."

He reached down again and handed Frank a small black codebook and a miniature tape recorder. "The recorder can be attached to a telephone or radio," he concluded.

Father and sons went over the principles of the decibel machine. When they had finished, the detective said, "Boys, you must guard this machine and the codebook carefully. These may be a lot more important on the second case I'm investigating."

"Is it connected with Iceland?" Joe asked.

"Very possibly. I want you to leave on tonight's Loftleidir flight to Reykjavik."

Frank made reservations immediately. After their father had left, Joe telephoned Chet.

"We're leaving for Kennedy International Airport at six," he said. "So bring your gear over to the house at five o'clock."

By four all was ready at the Hardy home. As the boys were locking their suitcases, a call came from police headquarters. Frank talked to the chief, and when he had finished, relayed the information to his brother. The prisoner had been identified. He was from New York City, a thug for hire, and seemed fearful about mentioning his employer.

"The other two made a getaway," Frank said. "They're probably in New York. Police there have been alerted."

Half an hour later Frank and Joe were amazed to see Chet's car pull up in front quietly and without backfiring. "Oh, oh, there's the reason," Joe said with a big grin. Frank looked out the window to see Iola at the wheel with Callie Shaw sitting beside her.

The Hardys ran out to greet them. Chet occupied the rear seat along with his suitcase, a flight bag, an extra heavy overcoat, and a small camera and a radio slung around his neck.

"I thought I'd better drive," Iola said with a dimpled smile, "because we wanted Chet to start his trip in good health."

"I just came along to say good-by," said Callie, looping her arm through Frank's.

"Chet, bring the stuff over here," Joe suggested. "We'll put it all in our car. Iola can drive it back and pick up the jalopy here."

Perspiring under the load of all his equipment, Chet deposited his baggage beside the Hardys' car.

When good-bys had been said to Mrs. Hardy and Aunt Gertrude, he reached down to pick up a black box. "Here, Iola, take this home. I won't need it. Frank and Joe have their short-wave radio."

Iola put the instrument aside, and the three boys loaded their belongings into the convertible.

"Got everything?" Joe asked.

"Yes," Frank replied.

The girls drove them to Bayport Airport in a matter of minutes. There they boarded a plane that arrived at Kennedy International Airport in ample time to sign in for the Icelandic trip.

After they had checked in with Loftleidir, Chet asked the ticket clerk, "Do you serve dinner on this flight?"

"Yes, sir. About an hour after you're airborne."

Chet rolled his eyes with a pleased expression. They headed for Gate 18, where a sleek jet-liner was taking on passengers. The boys entered through the front and walked toward the rear. Three seats were on either side of the aisle. Joe sat next to the window, while Chet slipped into the aisle seat, leaving Frank the place in the middle.

Then the plane's door was shut and it taxied to a runway. Buzzing like a bottled bumblebee, the huge craft lifted off and headed out across the sea toward the north.

Soon seat belts were removed and the boys tilted their seats back to enjoy the flight. By this time darkness had settled over the ocean beneath them.

The attractive stewardesses began bringing trays of food. Frank and Joe, being on the in-side, were served first.

"What, no more food left?" Chet asked with a worried expression.

The stewardess smiled down at him. "I'll be right back," she said.

When she returned, Chet started a conversation. "We're going to Iceland to see the Eskimos."

"Oh, really?" The dark-haired girl repressed a laugh. "But there aren't any Eskimos in Iceland."

"What?" Chet was perplexed.

Touching her fingers one at a time, the stewardess explained, "There are no Eskimos, no frogs, and no snakes in Iceland."

Joe grinned. "Then what *is* there in Iceland, Miss——?"

"Just call me Steina. You wouldn't remember my last name, it's too long."

The girl went on to say that there were glaciers and hidden people and night trolls—and, of course, ghosts. Then, before the boys could ask any other questions, she moved off to serve their fellow passengers.

"Hey, this is going to be an interesting trip!" Chet remarked, slicing through a juicy piece of steak.

"We'll have to learn more about those ghosts and night trolls," Frank said with a chuckle.

Steina returned later to remove their trays, but could not tarry to chat.

"She sure is good-looking," Chet whispered to Frank.

But Frank's mind was on the special equipment his father had supplied. He reached down into his flight bag tucked under the seat. The tape recorder was there in place. So was the code-book, slipped in tightly beside it. For no special reason, Frank pulled out the decibel counter. Suddenly a curious expression crossed his face.

"Holy crow, Joe, what's this?"

His brother's head was buried in a magazine.

Now he turned to look at the object in Frank's hand. "It's the decibel counter Dad gave us to—" He stopped short and his eyes grew wide. "Wait a minute—it's a radio!"

"Sure, it's mine," Chet put in. "I wonder how it got into your bag. Just before we left I gave it to Iola!"

CHAPTER III

An Ancient Custom

THE brothers stared at the radio they had brought by mistake. Without the decibel counter, the codebook was of no use! If Mr. Hardy had an urgent secret message, they could not receive it!

Frank shook his head. "Whew! This Icelandic case is starting off like a disaster! First the attempted kidnapping and now this!"

"I'm to blame for the whole thing," Chet muttered, crestfallen.

"No you're not," Joe said. He tried to console his friend. "It could have happened to anybody. The two cases look very much alike."

Frank realized that they had to get a message back home as soon as possible. He beckoned to the stewardess, who hastened up the aisle and bent over the seat.

"Steina," Frank said, "we have an emergency

on our hands. We must get a radio message back home."

"Emergency?"

"Yes," Joe added. "This is serious."

"All right. Come with me. We'll go to the captain."

Frank followed the pretty stewardess down the long aisle. When they reached the door of the crew's cabin, Steina knocked lightly and they entered. In the dim glow Frank saw four men who seemed to blend into the console of dials and instruments, which reached clear to the roof of the pilot's cabin.

The captain turned his eyes from the windshield and spoke to Steina in Icelandic. Then he switched to English and addressed Frank. "So you have an emergency, young man? . . . Yes, I can send a message by radio. What is it?"

The copilot handed Frank a pad and pencil. Quickly he printed the message to be delivered to his home in Bayport. He asked his parents to please get the black box from Iola Morton and send it to them at Keflavik Airport on the same flight next day.

Then Frank thanked the captain and the stewardess and returned to his seat. Soon the cabin's main lights were switched off and the passengers settled back for a short nap before the early dawn which would come about two o'clock.

The boys dozed fitfully until the lights came on

again and stewardesses busily went up and down the aisles serving breakfast. Frank looked out the window and gasped in amazement.

"Joe, Chet! Look at that!"

On the portside, rising out of the sea like a strange white world, loomed the snow-covered mountains of Greenland.

"Wow! That gives you the chills, doesn't it?" said Chet.

As the view of the great peaks inched by the wing tip, the boys talked about the huge island of Greenland, which seemed to spell adventure. Frank knew it was owned by Denmark, populated by Eskimos, and that there were several air bases on its shores.

"There's a Danish one called Narssarssuaq," he stated. He pulled a map from the seat pocket in front of him and opened it. "Here it is, look!"

"Boy, I'm glad I'm not an Eskimo," said Chet. "I could never spell a word like that!"

Their banter was interrupted by Steina, who brought them breakfast. Not long after they had eaten, the captain's voice crackled over the loud-speaker.

"We are on our descent to Keflavik. Please fasten your seat belts."

As the plane glided lower, the boys craned for a look at the country below. It had been born of volcanoes, and much of its surface was covered with lava and volcanic ash. Steaming hot springs lay next to its glaciers, and geysers spouted steam high into the air.

When the huge aircraft touched down, Frank swallowed hard to release the pressure in his ears.

"Exit through the front," Steina said. "Goodby, and have a good time in Iceland."

"We're on business," Chet said importantly. "But we'll try to have fun."

Lugging their hand baggage, Frank, Joe, and Chet climbed down the steps, breathing deeply of the crisp fresh air. Snow covered the airfield.

"Pretty bleak," Joe remarked as they hastened into a long, low building to be checked through customs.

An official stamped their passports and directed them to the back of the building, where a bus and taxis were waiting.

Frank talked to the driver standing beside the bus, and learned that Reykjavik was approximately thirty miles away. The bus would leave in twenty minutes.

The trio put their bags by the side of the building, then looked about the unusual landscape. A wide, black, barren valley swept off into the distance before rising abruptly to a bald, snow-clad mountain ridge.

"That's probably all made of lava," Joe declared, moving off a few paces to get a better look. Not far away an open jeep was parked on the side of the roadway, its hood lifted. A boy about their own age was tinkering with the motor.

Frank, Joe, and Chet casually walked over to him. "Find the trouble?" Frank asked.

The youth smiled at them. With a slight accent he replied, "Something's wrong with the carburetor."

"Let's take a look," Joe said. "Maybe we can help."

"Sure, be my guest."

The American colloquialism surprised the Hardys. "Oh, you've been in the States?" asked Frank.

"Yes, just got back a couple of days ago. My name is Gudmundur Bergsson." The boy wiped his hands on a piece of cloth and shook hands with the three. "Just call me Gummi." He told them that he was a student at a flying school in Tulsa, Oklahoma, and was learning to be a mechanic. "Now I'm home for spring vacation," he concluded.

Before Frank and Joe could examine the stalled motor, the loudspeaker blared: "Paging Frank and Joe Hardy!"

The boys looked up in surprise.

"Paging Frank and Joe Hardy," the announcer said again.

Joe started into the building, but Frank restrained him. "Not so fast, Joe. Nobody was to meet us here. Maybe it's another kidnapping attempt!"

"That's right," Chet chimed in. "We can't be too careful."

Gummi looked on, bewildered by the unusual conversation. "Somebody is trying to catch you guys?" he asked.

Frank nodded and said to Chet, "Just stroll inside and see who's paging us."

Chet left, returning a few minutes later. "A short, heavy-set guy with long blond hair and a mustache. Look, here he comes now!"

A square-looking man, his hair flowing, walked from the building. Frank and Joe ducked behind the jeep. The fellow looked right and left before climbing into a small foreign car. Then he drove off.

Frank glanced around for a taxi, but they had all gone. "I wish we could have followed him," he said disappointedly.

Gummi looked at the boys dubiously. "Hey, what's all this? Are you a couple of spies or something?"

Frank grinned. "We're detectives."

"No kidding."

"Look, it's a long story. We'll tell you later."

Gummi went to his tool kit without asking further questions, and before long, he and Frank had disassembled the carburetor.

"There's your trouble," Frank said, and wiped a piece of sludge from the intake.

Gummi laughed. "I can get you a mechanic's

job in Reykjavik any time you want," he said and started the engine. "Where are you fellows staying?"

"The Saga Hotel in Reykjavik," Joe replied.

"Want a ride into town?"

"Great!"

The boys got their bags and climbed into the jeep. On the way, they told Gummi about their search for Rex Hallbjornsson.

"Seems like looking for a needle in a haystack," the Icelandic boy commented. "There are two hundred thousand people on this island."

"How big is it?" Frank wanted to know.

"East to west about three hundred miles. Larger than Ireland, but we have not nearly as many inhabitants."

"What do people do for a living here?" Joe asked.

"Most of our income is derived from fishing," Gummi explained as he drove along a curving road hugging the rugged coastline. Not a tree was in sight. Only black lava formations.

Frank pointed to small piles of stone along the road. "What are these for?"

"They guided winter travelers in the olden days," Gummi replied. "And that village over there to the left is Hafnarfjordur."

As they entered the outskirts of Reykjavik, Gummi said, "When the first settlers came to this harbor, called a 'vik,' they saw steam coming from the ground in the distance. Thinking it was smoke, or 'reykja,' they called the place Reykjavik."

Gummi drove along a wide street lined with buildings which were faced with corrugated iron. The roofs were gaily painted in apple green, white, blue, or yellow.

"Quite a colorful place," Chet commented as he banged the side of the car with his right hand.

"Are you practicing karate, too?" Gummi asked. "It's the craze in our school right now. But Icelanders like wrestling better."

Finally they reached the center of town, where a small plaza was decorated with red-white-and-blue bunting and American flags.

Joe grinned. "Boy, they must have known we were coming!"

"If I didn't know better, I'd believe it." Gummi chuckled. "This is in honor of three U.S. astronauts who came here to study our lava surface, which is very similar to the terrain on the moon." He rounded a corner and pulled up in front of a modern white hotel located at the hub of three radiating roads. "Here you are."

The boys jumped out, unloaded their baggage, and thanked Gummi. He gave them his address and phone number. "Call me any time if you need help," he said. "I'll take you around in my jeep."

Frank and Joe occupied one room, and Chet an

adjoining one. After unpacking, they took the elevator to the eighth-floor restaurant for lunch.

"Well, masterminds," Chet asked between mouthfuls of broiled trout, "how are you going to find your boy Rex?"

"As soon as we're finished, let's look in the telephone book," Frank suggested.

When they consulted the directory, however, they stared at each other in confusion. "I can't make heads or tails of this," Joe stated. "It looks as if everything with 'son' at the end is a first name!"

"We'll give Gummi a call. Maybe he can explain," said Frank, and dialed their new friend's number. "Hey, what's all this crazy name business in Iceland?" he asked Gummi. "We can't find anybody by the name of Hallbjornsson under H."

Gummi laughed loudly. "People are listed by their first names in the telephone book," he said, and explained that the last name changed with every generation.

"Take me, for example," he said. "My father's name is Bergs Anderson. That makes my last name Bergsson. If I have a son, he'd be called Gudmundurson, and my daughter Gudmundurdottir. It's a holdover from the ancient Scandinavians. We still use it here."

"So we have to look under Rex, is that it?"

"Right. Good luck."

The boys thumbed through the directory. No Rex was listed.

"It looks as if we'll have to scan each page in search of Hallbjornsson," Joe said. "Rex might be a nickname."

About a half hour later Frank said, "Look! Here's an Ingrid Hallbjornsdottir. Maybe she's his sister."

They called Gummi again, who picked them up ten minutes later and drove them to the address. It turned out that the woman had no brothers and had never heard of Rex Hallbjornsson.

"Back to the phone book," Joe grumbled.

"Tell you what," Gummi said. "I'll help you look, and if we come up with any more leads, I'll call them from your hotel. This way we might save ourselves a few trips."

"Great idea, Gummi," Frank agreed. "You can question those people in Icelandic."

The boys drove back to the hotel and divided the work by getting three telephone directories. Each boy checked a different section. When they finished they had found two more Hallbjornsdottirs and one Hallbjornsson. Gummi called him. The man knew nobody by the name of Rex. Calls to the two women proved to be equally futile.

Since it was getting late, the Hardys said good

night to Gummi. "Would you take us to the airport tomorrow morning?" Frank asked. "We'll
have to pick up a package arriving on the early
flight."

"Sure thing. I'll be here on time."

Next morning after breakfast the boys went
to the lobby. Gummi was just coming through
the revolving door. "How's this package coming?
By air express?" he asked.

Frank said he did not know. They would in-
quire after the plane had landed.

At the airport the boys went to the waiting
room and watched the passengers stream in to
claim their baggage.

Suddenly Joe grabbed Frank's arm and turned
him toward the door. "Look who's here!"

"Can it be?" Chet blurted.

"Sure it is," Frank said excitedly. "Hey, Biff
Hooper!"

CHAPTER IV

Astronauts' Salute

GRINNING broadly, Biff Hooper greeted the
Hardys and Chet, then handed Frank a little
black box which he carried under his arm.

"Oh boy, am I glad to see this!" Frank said.
"Thanks, Biff."

"Your dad phoned me," Biff said. "He didn't
want to send it by air express." Then he squared
his broad shoulders. "Besides, he thought you
might need me!"

"That sounds ominous," Joe stated. "Does Dad
think there'll be any trouble?"

"Couldn't say," Biff replied, glancing about the
airport building.

Frank beckoned to Gummi, who had been
standing in the background. After introductions
were made, Biff claimed his baggage and the five
went out to the jeep. On the ride back to Reyk-

javik, Frank asked Biff if he had noticed anyone following him.

"No, I didn't see anybody."

Back at the hotel, Biff moved into Chet's room. After he had freshened up, Gummi suggested lunch at the Hotel Borg. "It is in the center of town on the plaza," he said, "and if you like sea-food—"

"That's for me!" Chet said quickly.

"Okay, let's go."

They were downtown in no time at all, and after Gummi parked the car, they entered the ground-floor restaurant, which looked old-fash-ioned by American standards. The waiters were young, no older than the Hardys, and they moved about with ease and aplomb. Gummi ordered a seafood tray and mentioned something else to the waiter in Icelandic.

"*Yow, yow!*" the waiter replied, grinning.

"What's *yow, yow?*" Chet wanted to know.

"It means yes, yes, spelled *ja*," Gummi told him.

"I knew I'd learn Icelandic eventually—*yow, yow, yow!*"

"And don't forget, no is *nei*."

The waiter brought a small plate of yellowish dried fish, cut into small bits.

"It's *hardfisk*," Gummi explained, "and a spe-cialty of Iceland. You put butter on it and eat it like this."

Chet put a piece in his mouth and started to chew. "Tastes like wood splinters," he complained.

"Keep chewing," Gummi advised.

"Hm! Now it tastes good—it melts in your mouth."

When everyone had tried the *hardfisk*, the waiter arrived with a platter of ten different kinds of seafood; sild herring, small shrimps, caviar and other delicacies.

"Iceland is not a bad place for a detective case," Joe remarked. Just then they heard the sound of horns. The boys looked out the window.

"I think the astronauts are driving by," Gummi said.

Half rising from the seats of their booth, they looked out onto the street. A car came by, with two small American flags fluttering at the front fenders.

"They're our astronauts, all right," Frank said. "I recognize them."

Three men were riding in the back seat. The one in the middle held his head low, with his cap well down over his eyes.

"That one must be Major Kenneth McGeorge," Frank said. "They're probably on their way back to Keflavik for their trip home, now that they know what the moon looks like."

"Next trip for them the moon," Joe said.

"I know they'll make it," Gummi said. "They're great guys."

Chet Morton, as usual, ate more than anyone else. When he had finished the last morsel of shrimp, Gummi Bergsson said, "In regard to your insurance case, I have a suggestion. You should see Anders Sigurdsson at the Foreign Office. Tell him your problem. He might be able to help."

The Foreign Office was located on a small hill near the center of town. The two-story building looked like an oversized bungalow. Gummi waited outside with Chet and Biff while the Hardy boys entered. They were ushered to an office on the second floor, where a short, smiling, gray-haired man greeted them. The boys told him their problem.

"So you're looking for Rex Hallbjornsson," the man mused. "I have never heard of him, but that's not unusual. I would suggest that you put an advertisement in our five daily newspapers."

"Five newspapers in a city of seventy-five thousand?" Frank asked in amazement.

"That's right. Icelanders like to read. In fact, there is no illiteracy in our country. Also, these papers are sent to other towns on the island."

"We'll follow your suggestion, Mr. Sigurdsson," Frank said. "Thank you very much."

"Not at all. Come back if I can be of more help."

Frank and Joe left the building, stopping at the front door to survey the small city which lay before them. Traffic kept to the right side of the road, as in America, and the narrow streets were filled mostly with European-made autos.

Frank scanned the view from left to right, where the road led down to the waterfront. Suddenly he backed into the doorway. "Joe, duck!"

A German-made Taunus car drove slowly toward the front of the building. Its driver had long blond hair and a flowing mustache! The man pulled to the side of the road and scanned Gummi's jeep.

"That's the fellow who had us paged at the airport!" Frank whispered.

"He must have found out what hotel we're staying at and is trailing us," Joe said.

The man's eyes went up the long walk to the door of the Foreign Office, but he could not see the Hardys.

"Something's fishy," Frank stated. "Maybe he has something to do with the guys who were trying to kidnap me."

"Never can tell," Joe replied. "We'd better be careful until we find out who he really is."

As they watched, the Taunus moved off slowly, turned the corner into Austur Straeti, and disappeared.

The Hardys hurried to the jeep.

"Did you see that guy?" Joe asked Gummi.

"Sure did. Come on. We'll follow him."

Traffic was heavy, and soon the Taunus was out of sight. "He might have driven down to the harbor area," Gummi said. "Let's try that." He made a few turns but could not pick up the man's trail.

"He gave us the shake," Gummi said in American lingo. "Where do you want to go now?"

"I saw a newspaper office at the head of Austur Straeti," Frank replied. "Let's go back. I want to place an ad in all the local newspapers."

"Okay, I'll take you to each one of them. Hey, this detective stuff is great!"

It took the rest of the afternoon to place the ads in the five dailies. Frank kept it short. *Will Rex Hallbjornsson please contact the Hardy boys at the Saga Hotel and collect insurance money due him.* Gummi translated it into Icelandic.

"Do you think it's wise to mention money?" Biff Hooper asked.

Frank shrugged. "It might be the only way to get him to reply."

"Sure, what have we got to lose?" Joe said.

On the way back to the hotel, Biff pointed to a cluster of huge tanks sitting on the hill in the center of Reykjavik. "What a place to put gas tanks!"

Gummi laughed. "Gas tanks? Those are filled with hot water."

"What for?"

Gummi explained that the tanks were located over boiling springs of water, which surged up from the depths of the earth. "The hot water is stored and piped into every home in Reykjavik," he said. "We don't have any heating problem here."

"Quite a system!" Biff remarked.

"And you're always in hot water!" Chet quipped.

"Throw him out!" said Biff.

"Careful of me," Chet replied, and banged his seat with a karate chop.

"What a clown!" Biff said, laughing.

Gummi had some chores to do for his father and left the Bayporters at the hotel. That evening after dinner the Hardys unlimbered their radio, because they expected a message from their father.

"Don't forget there's a four-hour difference in time," Frank said. "I have a hunch Dad won't transmit until night, when the atmosphere is clear."

The boys fiddled with the set, tuning in various stations. They were rewarded at midnight when they received a coded broadcast from Mr. Hardy. Frank quickly attached the decibel unit to the radio and started the conversation.

Mr. Hardy talked about the opening baseball game in the major leagues. "The Yankees scored three in the ninth to win their game," he said. "With good pitching they should have a great season."

It sounded casual enough. The boys had decided not to reveal their suspicions concerning the blond stranger. They would wait until they had some constructive evidence.

When Mr. Hardy signed off, Frank went to work on the decibel counter. The peaks, visibly recorded on the tape of the machine, were transposed into letters.

Then Joe took out the codebook. "Here, give me a pencil, Frank!"

Frank pulled one out of his pocket, and his brother began to decode the message word by word. At the end of the first sentence, Frank and Joe gasped in amazement. One of the U.S. astronauts missing! It couldn't be true. But there were the words: *Ken McGeorge has been lost in Iceland!*

CHAPTER V

The Boiling Pit

THE news of Ken McGeorge's disappearance hit the boys like an avalanche. Their hearts beat wildly as they continued to decode Mr. Hardy's message:

Keep your eyes open for any clues to McGeorge. Chet and Biff must be sworn to complete secrecy. Space program at stake.

Mr. Hardy added that he had obtained clearance from Washington for his sons and their friends to help.

Chet had been standing with his mouth open. Now he blurted, "But—but—we just saw the three astronauts on their way to Keflavik!"

Frank snapped his fingers. "Remember the fellow in the middle? He had his hat pulled down low over his face. I'll bet he was a stand-in for McGeorge!"

"That's right," said Joe. "Obviously the government doesn't want the news to leak out. It might jeopardize the whole NASA program."

"What a mystery you got yourselves into this time!" Biff Hooper exclaimed.

"Now the pieces fall into place," Frank said. "Dad must have been working on this case before we left. Remember, Joe, the mysterious call from the White House?"

"Right. And those two men who visited him in the middle of the night were probably government officials!" Joe briefly told Biff and Chet about the occurrences in the Hardy home.

"He went to Texas just before we flew to Iceland," Frank concluded. "Probably checking out McGeorge's co-workers and friends."

"If we're going to find the major in Iceland," Joe said, "we'd better work fast. If he was kidnapped, they might force information from him."

"Now we're all going to take a pledge of secrecy," Frank said. He slapped his hand on the table. Chet came forward with his, then Joe, and finally Biff.

"Not a word to anybody, through thick and thin," Frank said.

"Gosh, who knows what'll happen to us!" Chet said worriedly.

"Whatever does," Biff stated with a grim jaw, "nobody will ever learn anything from us!"

Suddenly the radio crackled again, and another

message came from Mr. Hardy, saying that the astronaut had disappeared on the lava plain near Reykjavik.

"We'll go there tomorrow," Frank said. "Maybe we'll find a clue."

The four companions were up early the next morning, and Frank phoned Gummi. He tried to conceal his excitement. "How would you like to take us around today, Gummi?"

"Sure. Where to?"

"The tour the astronauts made on the lava plain near here sounds interesting."

"Okay. I'll check the newspapers to find the exact route. It was well publicized."

An hour later he arrived outside the hotel, beeped his horn, and the Americans climbed into the jeep.

A smooth highway led south out of town, but soon the Icelandic youth turned onto a rugged road leading into a valley of breath-taking desolation. Gaunt, snow-capped mountains rose on either side, and the valley was black with oddly shaped chunks of lava.

"Did the astronauts get out and walk around here?" asked Frank as the jeep bounced along.

"That's what they came for," Gummi replied. "This place is said to resemble the moon's surface."

"I can just see moon people hiding out there now," Biff quipped.

"We have our own hidden people in Iceland," Gummi replied.

"Hidden people?" Biff asked.

Frank recalled Steina's remark on the plane. "Not to mention ghosts!"

Gummi turned in surprise. "You know about the ghosts?"

"Not much," Frank admitted.

"I've got my special ghost," Gummi declared. "He travels with me all the time."

"Who's he?" Joe asked.

"My grandfather."

"What superstition!" Chet said, and Gummi did not look pleased.

"It's a fact!"

"No offense," Chet muttered.

The road meandered to avoid large black masses of lava. Gummi fought the wheel to keep the jeep on course over the rugged terrain.

"This looks as if it leads to nowhere," Frank commented.

"What about these hidden people?" Joe asked.

Gummi explained the Icelandic belief. "They live in little green hillocks, and if you look carefully, you might see them peering out at you. They wear bright-colored clothes, and their faces are pale and peaceful."

Chet shuddered a little bit and looked about the eerie valley. Suddenly he leaned forward and gripped Gummi's shoulder.

"Hey-y-y! I just saw one!"

"Saw what?" asked Frank.

"Something moved behind one of those rocks!"

Gummi hit the brakes, and the boys jumped down onto the road.

"Chet, you're letting your imagination run away with you," Joe said with a grin.

"I'm not kidding!" the stout boy replied. "I really saw someone."

Frank and Joe exchanged glances. Maybe there was something in Chet's story! They could not afford to take any chances, knowing that the blond man had been trailing them.

"Okay. Let's see where the ghost appeared," Frank suggested.

The boys followed Chet over the abrasive surface toward a large chunk of lava which looked something like a troll bent over.

Gingerly Chet stepped around it. Nobody was there!

"Maybe he went over that way!" Chet said, pointing to the next hiding place behind another rock fragment.

The boys continued their search, circling half a dozen lava rocks. Suddenly Joe cried out as he stepped into a crevice. Wincing, he pulled his right leg out and danced around in pain.

"Wow! I scraped my shin!"

"You must be careful climbing around here," Gummi warned.

Joe stepped into a crevice

"All right, Chet, are you satisfied now?" Joe asked, annoyed by the accident.

"Okay, but I really—"

"Baloney!" Joe replied, hobbling back to the jeep.

Gummi smiled to himself as he started off again. As the road wound higher along the mountain, it grew soggier because of the recent melted snow. Soon they passed a broad lake which lay gray and forbidding in a small pass.

"This whole place gives me the creeps," Biff said. "I wish I could see some trees!"

"That's what I like about Oklahoma—the trees," Gummi declared. "There were trees in Iceland centuries ago, but the early settlers cut them down.

"Well, here we are," he said finally as he pulled off the road onto a small trail with several inches of snow.

"Somebody's been here before," Joe observed, pointing to tire tracks which led in and out.

Soon they came to the place where the other vehicle had stopped. Footprints led from the spot over the brow of a small rise, but they did not come back!

Beyond the rise a jet of steam, hissing like a gigantic snake, rose high into the air.

"That's coming from the sulfur pit over there," Gummi explained, "and the steam hole, too."

Joe leaped out first and ran up over the brow of the hill.

"Careful!" Gummi warned. "You don't want to be cooked in sulfur!"

Frank jumped down from the jeep and surveyed the terrain. He lingered behind the others so he could look for clues without being questioned.

Several thoughts ran through his mind, "How could one astronaut have disappeared? No doubt the three were accompanied by government officials. Major McGeorge must have separated from the rest and been waylaid. But how could he have been carried off without anyone noticing it, and by whom and where to?"

Finding no clues, Frank trailed after the other four. When he reached the rise, he looked down at the pit. It was about six feet across, bubbling and burping from the bowels of the earth.

The atmosphere was filled with the smell of sulfur, some of which came from the steam shooting out of a huge pipe with an earsplitting roar.

Frank suddenly noticed that only Gummi, Biff, and Chet were in sight. He raced toward the trio, standing beside the pit. No use shouting, nobody could hear. Frank glanced about wildly. A black leather glove lay close to the edge of the bubbling sulfur. Footprints were nearby.

A chill ran down Frank's spine as he looked from the glove to his friends. Gummi suddenly caught on. His face took on a look of terror. He gestured at Frank and the other boys, and all had the same thought. Where was Joe? Had he fallen into the pit?

CHAPTER VI

Tricked in the Sky

FRANTICALLY the boys searched for Joe. Each shouted at the top of his lungs, but the thundering steam bursting out of the pipe like a hundred roaring jet engines muted every other sound.

Frank suddenly gesticulated toward the standpipe, with an expression of utter relief on his face. Joe Hardy emerged from behind it. He hastened over to them as Chet picked up the glove from the snow, and they all moved off to a distance where they could hear each other.

"Holy crow!" Frank sighed. "Joe, you had us scared to death. We thought you'd fallen into the pit."

"Sorry about that," Joe replied. He had bent down to examine the rusted bolts at the foot of the standpipe. "The sulfur in that steam is corroding everything," he said. "Someday the whole pipe is going to blow right up into the air."

"I wonder whom the glove belongs to," Gummi mused.

The Hardys and their two friends were thinking the same thought, but did not speak out in front of the Icelander. Did Ken McGeorge drop it while being kidnapped?

The brothers lagged behind to talk in private, while the others returned to look at the sulfur pit. Frank said, "It stands to reason, Joe, that this place has been searched thoroughly by the authorities."

"That's right. They would have found the glove long before we did."

"The only answer," Frank went on, "is that the glove was dropped recently."

"By Major McGeorge?" Joe asked.

"It's a puzzler," Frank admitted. He walked over to Gummi and asked when it had snowed last.

"Early yesterday morning," Gummi replied.

The split-second glance that Frank exchanged with his brother was significant. If it were the astronaut's glove, he must have returned to the pit the night before. But why?

The boys stayed a few minutes longer to look at the sulfur pit and the steam blowhole.

Gummi explained that there were many such phenomena over the entire island. "Iceland probably popped out of the sea just like Surtsey," he said, referring to the underwater volcano which had boiled up out of the sea a few years ago, causing the formation of a small island off the south coast.

Frank took the leather glove from Chet and put it in his pocket. It was a clue that might prove significant, but they could not give it to the police without tipping their hand.

First thing to do now, Frank thought, was to check the lone set of footmarks, which did not return to the spot where they had started. He and Joe followed them for a way, and realized that they were double prints, leading in a roundabout way to the road about two hundred yards distant. Apparently two men had approached the sulfur pit, one behind the other, the second one stepping in the first one's footprints.

"This is fantastic," Joe remarked. "Maybe we should tell the police about this right away."

"No," Frank replied. "Let's first examine this glove and find out if it's GI."

"And how are we going to do that?"

"We'll have to get another one from the U.S. base in Keflavik. Then we can compare the leather under a microscope."

The Hardys trudged back to the jeep, where the others were already waiting. As they drove back over the bumpy road toward the highway south of Reykjavik, fear gnawed at Frank. Had the astronaut's captors disposed of him in the sulfur pit?

Gummi dropped them at their hotel and left for home. At lunch the Hardys talked about their plans with Chet and Biff.

"Listen, fellows," Frank said. "You two stay here and watch out for any suspicious characters, while Joe and I take a taxi to Keflavik. We'd like to let Gummi in on this, but we'd better not."

After explaining that they would try to find a glove of similar manufacture, Frank and Joe left.

Arriving at Keflavik, they obtained permission to enter the base. Frank spoke to a captain in charge of general issue and asked if he might borrow a leather glove used by officers. The captain was amazed at the request, but after the Hardys identified themselves as American detectives working on an insurance case, the officer gave them a glove.

"We'll return it," Frank promised.

"That's all right. You can keep it."

"Thanks, Captain."

Back at the hotel, Frank asked the desk clerk if he could direct them to a medical laboratory.

"Anybody sick?" the man asked in surprise.

"No," Joe replied. "We have another reason."

The clerk looked at them curiously, riffled through a sheaf of addresses, and came up with one.

Although it was late in the afternoon, Frank

and Joe took a chance. They called the lab and found that it was still open. "We would like to borrow a microscope," Frank explained. He was told that no instruments could be taken from the premises, but was invited to come over and use one.

"We close at six," the man said in perfect English.

"We'll be right there," Frank replied.

The Hardys took a taxi to the laboratory, which was located at the center of town, not far from the Foreign Office. A courteous technician greeted them and directed the boys to a small room. A microscope stood on a table to the left. The man asked if they would be examining germ cultures.

"Oh no," Joe said with a smile. "We're just comparing two pieces of leather."

"Go ahead," said the technician and left.

The research did not take long. First they examined the outside leather. Each glove proved to be of the same general quality. The stitching was made by similar machines, and the woolen linings were identical.

"That does it," Frank said. "This was lost by a military man."

"Should we tell the police now?" Joe asked.

But Frank was adamant about following their father's instruction. "Not yet, Joe. Not yet."

The Hardys thanked the lab technician and

left. Returning to the hotel, they found Biff and Chet eagerly waiting for them in the lobby. Biff waved a letter in his hand.

"Frank, Joe, you got an answer to your ad!"

Frank took the envelope and tore it open. It was from Reykjavik's leading newspaper, and inside was another letter. He read the message. It had come from Akureyri, a city on the north coast.

A man signing his name Rex Hallbjornsson said that he was the one they were looking for. He requested that the boys come to see him.

"That was easy," Chet commented. "Our first swing's a home run!"

"Too easy," Joe replied.

"I think you're right," his brother said. "We've got to be careful about this."

Chet scratched his head. "Always suspicious."

"Just cautious," Joe said.

Biff agreed with the Hardys. "After all, it's kind of fishy that the guy won't come here. If somebody offered *me* money, I wouldn't mind picking it up myself!"

It was agreed that Frank and Joe would fly to Akureyri the next day, leaving Chet and Biff at the hotel to guard their radio and decoding equipment.

"I'm going to Flugfelag Islands," Frank announced after breakfast the next morning.

"What?" asked Chet.

Frank handed him a travel folder which he had picked up at the desk.

"Flugfelag Islands," Chet read. "I wonder where they are."

"Listen, dummy," Biff Hooper said, giving Chet a mock stiff-arm, which his buddy parried with a karate chop. "Flugfelag Islands means Iceland Airlines."

"Attaboy, Biff!" Joe grinned. "You're learning the language."

The Hardys recalled seeing a Flugfelag office in the hotel lobby. Joe had noticed a dark-haired woman behind the desk the day before, but when the Hardys went to the office, it was empty. A few seconds later a man came in and sat down.

Frank approached him. "We'd like to take a plane to Akureyri," he said. "Today."

"Sorry," the man replied with a slight accent. "There are no scheduled flights to Akureyri until tomorrow. I would suggest that if you want to go today, you take a small private plane—it is cheaper, too."

"Will you make the arrangements?" Joe asked.

"Of course. What are your names?"

When the boys had given him all the information, the man said, "Be at the Flugfelag terminal at twelve noon. It is quite near the hotel, you know."

"Okay," Frank said. "Please charge it to our room." He gave the man the number. Then the boys hastened to the elevator and went back up-stairs.

Chet was sprawled on Frank's bed, while Biff sat looking out the window. "I'd like to see Aku-reyri, too," he grumbled. "Can't we just leave Chet here to guard the equipment?"

"What's the big idea?" the stout boy said, ris-ing. "I can tackle two, perhaps three guys, but no more. And they might send half a dozen here, you know!" He cleaved the air with a couple of karate strokes.

"All right, I'll stay," said Biff. "But get back soon!"

"Sure." Frank grinned. "And just so your job won't be too demanding, I'll put this in the safe!" He took the codebook and went down to the lobby.

At eleven-thirty Frank and Joe stood in front of the Saga, where a taxi drove up to get them. Ten minutes later they reached the airfield. As they stepped inside the terminal building, they were met by the agent.

"I thought I would be here to help," he said. "Follow me." He led them out onto the field, where they saw a small twin-engine plane warm-ing up.

"The pilot does not speak very good English," the agent explained, pulling open the cabin door against the propeller's slipstream. "But he will bring you to Akureyri in less than an hour."

Frank and Joe climbed in, fastened their seat belts, and glanced toward the pilot's cabin. The door was shut. Outside, the agent waved to them, then the plane taxied for take-off. Soon they were airborne, and the boys looked down on the bright-colored roofs of Reykjavik.

"Well, let's find out where Akureyri is, exactly," said Frank after a while and pulled a map of Iceland from his pocket. Both studied it, then sat back to watch the mountainous terrain unfolding before them.

Frank, who was sitting next to the window on the starboard side, glanced up at the sun.

"Hey, Joe, this is funny. We're supposed to be heading north, aren't we?"

"Sure," Joe replied. "That's where Akureyri is."

"But look! We're going east. See the position of the sun?"

According to the boy's reckoning, they were flying in the wrong direction. Frank's fears were confirmed when he glanced down and saw the jagged south coast of Iceland far beneath them.

"What's going on with that pilot?" Joe asked, annoyed.

"We'd better find out."

The boys slipped from their seats and approached the cabin. Joe opened the door and cried out in alarm. The pilot was their blond enemy!

"Where are you taking us?" Joe demanded.

The man motioned the boys away. "No speak!"

"Of course you speak English!" Frank said angrily, realizing that every pilot had to be versed in that language.

Joe pulled his brother out of the cabin so they could speak without being overheard.

"Frank, what are we going to do about this guy? You know what's happening—we're being kidnapped."

"We'll have to take over," Frank replied tersely.

Both boys were skillful pilots. Although they did most of their flying in single-engine planes, they felt sure they could handle the twin-engine job.

"Where'll we land?" Joe asked.

"Once we have control of the plane, we can radio Reykjavik for instructions," Frank stated, glancing out the window. Below, a huge glacier came into view. The boys had studied the map carefully and realized that they were over Vatnajokull, the largest and most forbidding glacier in all of Iceland.

"We'll go in and I'll drag him from behind the wheel," Frank said. "You grab the yoke on the copilot's side. Okay?"

"Let's go!"

They approached the pilot. Frank reached forward to get a headlock on him, but the man swung a quarter way around and clipped him on the chin. As Frank staggered back, the portside engine began to sputter. Seconds later the starboard engine conked out. And all at once the pilot spoke perfect English!

"Let me handle this!" he said. "We are going to have to land on the glacier!"

CHAPTER VII

A Harrowing Blizzard

STILL groggy from the blow on the chin, Frank dropped into the copilot's seat. He grasped the wheel as Joe, his eyes flashing anger over the brazen kidnapping, swung a hard right at the pilot. The fist caught him at the side of the jaw, and the man slumped unconscious.

Wind whistled eerily over the wings as the plane glided toward the gigantic sheet of white ice beneath them.

Closer and closer it angled down toward Vatna-jokull. Now the boys saw that much of the glacier was serrated with jagged knife-edged ridges. Small hills of ice and crevasses came into sharp focus.

"Frank, we'll never make it!" Joe cried out.

His brother sat grim-lipped and silent. Skill-fully he guided the descent so as not to lose fly-ing speed. His feet firmly on the rudder bar,

Frank banked the plane and headed for what appeared to be a smoother spot in the sloping glacier about half a mile away.

Landing on the slope would be tricky enough for the most skilled pilot. With the wheels now inches above what proved to be bumpy ice, Frank pulled back on the yoke.

The whiteness rushed up to meet them! Their plane bounced with a terrifying crunch, lifted into the air, and settled again with tires squealing.

The aircraft slid back a few feet before finally coming to a halt. Joe felt limp. "Thanks, Frank," was all he could say. "That was the greatest!"

Both boys felt lucky to come out of the crash landing alive, but were furiously angry with the man responsible for their dire predicament.

The pilot was now conscious. He lifted his head and looked about dazedly.

"Okay now," Joe said, shaking him by the shoulder. "Who are you? And what's your racket?"

"Help—we need help," was the weak reply.

"You know the ropes!" Frank said impatiently. "Get on the radio and call for aid!" He climbed out of the copilot's seat and looked about the plane.

Meanwhile, the man picked up the microphone and slowly transmitted their position. There was silence for a minute or two, then he signed off.

"Someone will come for us," he reported.

"Okay—but that doesn't explain who you are!"

Frank resumed their interrogation. But the man remained mute, shaking his head as if still in a stupor.

The Hardys were both aggravated and frightened. "Here we are, wrecked on top of the world," Joe muttered, "and this dummy won't tell us anything!"

He pulled the man from his seat and pushed him to the plane's door. Frank frisked the pilot to make sure he had no weapons.

The icy air blanketing the glacier hit them like a bucket full of cold water as they stepped onto the slippery surface. They looked the plane over. Both propellers were bent, and even if the engines could have been repaired, a take-off looked impossible.

Despite continued questioning by the Hardys, the pilot remained silent. As they were about to give up, they suddenly heard the distant sound of a helicopter.

"Wow! That chopper came pretty fast!" Joe said, shielding his eyes to watch the craft hover over the glacier.

"Good night!" Frank exclaimed. "It's only a two-seater job!"

"Well, you know who goes out first—in handcuffs. Old blondie here is getting a ride to jail!"

Frank looked at their sullen kidnapper, whose shifty eyes glanced up at the rescue craft. "You'll talk when the Reykjavik police get hold of you," he said. "They'll find out what's behind all this hocus-pocus."

The helicopter landed close to the airplane, and a man of medium height hopped down. He had black hair, rugged features, and a long nose which looked anything but Scandinavian. He began speaking immediately in a foreign tongue.

"Can you speak English, sir?" Frank interrupted.

"A little."

"This joker tried to kidnap us, but the engines failed. You don't happen to have a pair of handcuffs, do you?"

"No. But I have some rope."

The man reached into the seat of the helicopter and produced a length of stout twine. Frank bound the wrists of their captive.

"We'll press charges when we get to Reykjavik ourselves," Frank went on. "Please turn this man over to the police and come back for us as soon as you can."

With a smart salute, the chopper pilot pushed the prisoner into the helicopter, then climbed into his seat and took off.

"Am I glad to get rid of blondie!" Joe said. "That guy gave me the creeps."

"Pretty evil-looking character," his brother agreed, then added, "Just to double-check, I'm calling Reykjavik on the radio and tell them the helicopter's coming back."

The boys climbed back into the plane, closing the door to keep out the glacier air.

Then Frank tried to activate the radio. No luck! "Hey, Joe, look at this!"

"What's the matter?" his brother asked, coming forward along the sloping cabin.

"The radio's conked out!"

All at once a chill of realization surged over the Hardys. The pilot had sabotaged the set! Frank quickly examined it. The frequency crystal was missing.

"I don't believe he sent a rescue message at all," Frank stated. "We've really been had, Joe!"

"You mean the helicopter was following us all the time?"

"I'm afraid so. Now we're in a real pickle!"

Perspiration stood out on Joe's forehead. "What'll we do, Frank?"

"Look for the part. Our blond Viking might have dropped it onto the ice when we weren't looking."

The boys hopped out of the plane again and searched the icy surface, but in vain! Dark clouds sped in from the south, dropping lower and lower.

"Now we're in for it!" Joe muttered. He looked up to see snowflakes land on the disabled plane.

"Looks as if it might be a bad storm," Frank said, and the boys climbed back inside the cabin.

Before long, the snow fell so thickly that they

could not see three feet ahead. The wind rose, and by nightfall the Hardys were caught in a howling glacial blizzard. At the same time, the temperature dropped sharply.

"We didn't come dressed for anything like this," Frank said, shivering. He glanced about for some extra clothing. Joe found a repair locker. In it were some tools and a greasy overall.

"You put that on," Frank said.

"What about you?"

"Don't worry. We'll have to start a fire to keep us warm."

"And burn the plane up?"

"We'll have to take that chance."

Although the remaining fuel in the tank might have provided the much-needed heat, Frank and Joe decided against using the highly volatile gasoline. Instead, they opened the door a crack for ventilation, then tore off bits of interior woodwork with which they built a small fire on the floor of the aircraft.

The resultant warmth proved to be adequate. "At least we won't *freeze* to death now," Joe said with a wry grin.

"We'll take turns tending this fire all night," Frank suggested, glancing out the window. Nothing could be seen but the thick covering of snow and the crack in the door revealed only the blackness of the storm's fury.

The boys agreed to sit up in shifts, feeding

the fire with whatever material they could find to burn.

Near dawn, the howling winds abated, and Joe tore one of the passenger's seats apart for fuel. Suddenly he let out a cry of delight.

"Frank, I found it!"

CHAPTER VIII

Something Fishy

ROUSED from a fitful sleep, Frank sat up groggily and rubbed his eyes. "What did you say, Joe? You found something?"

"Sure, look at this!" Joe held up a square-shaped metal piece about the size of a nickel. "The frequency crystal for the radio. It was thrown behind one of the seats!"

The news electrified Frank into direct action. Stepping over the glowing embers of their fire, he hastened to the front of the plane. After he had replaced the part, the radio was in perfect condition. Within seconds, Frank made contact with the radio tower at Reykjavik.

After he had told his story, the dispatcher said that an Icelandic coast guard helicopter would come to their aid.

Frank sent another message to be relayed to

Chet and Biff at the Saga Hotel, saying everything was okay.

Despite the cold, the boys jumped from the plane into the deep snow. They trudged about, packing down a place for the helicopter to land. An hour later it came zooming low over the glacier.

The Hardys waved furiously to attract the pilot's attention. In minutes he had the craft on the glacier and stepped out to meet them.

"Are you hurt?" he asked.

"No, we're all right," Frank said.

"Pretty nasty accident. You were lucky to come out alive. Did you rent your plane in Reykjavik?"

Briefly Frank related what had happened, and how their kidnapper had gotten away.

"That was not one of our rescue copters," the airman stated.

"We figured that," Joe replied.

The pilot got into the copter, with the Hardys following.

"Can we ask you a favor?" Frank said when the craft was airborne.

"What is it?"

"Could you take us directly to Akureyri?"

The man frowned. "Why Akureyri?"

Joe explained that they were American detectives on the trail of a Rex Hallbjornsson who had answered their ad with a letter postmarked Akureyri.

The pilot grinned. "I suppose our government can do a favor for American detectives." With that, he wheeled the craft northward.

Soon the glacier gave way to rolling meadows, with patches of green showing through the light covering of snow.

"Look sharp," the pilot said, "and let me know if you see any polar bears."

"Polar bears?" Frank asked. "I didn't know there were any in Iceland."

"Usually not," the man replied. He explained that the winter had been severe, causing a huge tongue of ice to extend from Greenland around the north coast of Iceland. It curved down along the eastern shore of the country.

"Several polar bears were carried down on the ice and they climbed onto our island. One has been caught, but some are still roaming around, as far as the west coast. They have killed sheep, and one farmer had to flee for his life."

Frank and Joe kept looking for bears, but all they saw were several small settlements with sod huts and flocks of sheep grazing on the greening pastures.

Every now and then the boys spotted small ponies. When they questioned the pilot, he said, "Ponies used to be our chief means of transportation. We still use them a lot here. Icelandic ponies are strong and durable."

The north coast came into view and the airman

pointed to a bay that cut deep inland. "There's Akureyri!"

Shortly afterward, he landed the craft in a field not far from the center of town, and the boys got out.

"Good luck to you," the pilot said, waving good-by. "I'll make a report to the coast guard in Reykjavik."

First, Frank and Joe found a drugstore where they purchased shaving equipment. The next stop was a small hotel, where they registered, cleaned up, and had breakfast in their room.

Tired out from their harrowing experience, they decided to sleep for a couple of hours. But when they awakened, it was already growing dark.

Frank was annoyed with himself. "We should have had the clerk buzz us earlier," he said.

"Well," Joe replied, stretching luxuriously, "Rex Hallbjornsson probably works, and wouldn't have been home anyhow."

The boys ate supper in the hotel dining room, then set out to find the elusive Icelander. His address was a small one-family house, made of aging brick and plaster, with a steep corrugated roof. It was located on a side street, across from a fish factory.

As they approached, Frank held his nose. "Phew!" he said. "They must be making fertilizer in there!"

Joe knocked and the door was opened by a

middle-aged woman, who spoke fairly good English. Yes, Hallbjornsson lived there, she said, adding that another American had been looking for him, too.

"Another?" Frank asked, perplexed.

"Yes, come this way," the landlady said, disregarding his query, and ushered the boys down the hall into a small room. Seated in a well-worn easy chair beside a small cot was a man, completely bald. His blue eyes blinked as he stared at the callers.

"We're Frank and Joe Hardy," Frank said. "Are you Rex Hallbjornsson?"

"*Ja.*" In halting English, Hallbjornsson said he was both excited and glad to see the boys. He motioned for them to sit on his cot, then made a quick phone call in a foreign tongue.

When he returned, Frank said, "We understand you're a seaman."

"You were shipwrecked, too," Joe added. "Pretty lucky man to be alive."

Hallbjornsson nodded and proceeded to tell them a long story about his travels to Europe. None of the details agreed with the information their father had given them. And the man did not have the weather-beaten face of a sailor.

"I was shipwrecked in Spain," he went on, "and hit my head on the gunwale of the rescue boat. Then I had—what do you say?—amnesia. For five years I wandered, until one day in Turkey—"

"That was when you worked for the Greek shipping company," Joe put in, embroidering the man's false tale.

"*Ja.* You know about that?"

Frank nodded and pursued Joe's tack. "Then you went to Syria, and finally back to Iceland, right?"

"Good. I am glad you know the details," Hallbjornsson said. "That will make it easier for me to collect. How much money do I get?"

"Fifty thousand dollars," Frank replied.

The man's eyes bulged greedily. "Do you have it with you?"

"No, we don't have any money with us," Frank replied. "Naturally, we'll have to make a report to the insurance company first. But if you're the right man, you'll get what you're entitled to receive."

"*Ja, ja,*" the man murmured. "Make it soon. You see how I am living here in this cheap room. And I am getting old."

The boys said good-by, stepped out into the hall, and made their way to the front of the house. They tried to find the landlady to question her about the other American, but she was nowhere in sight.

It was pitch dark when they stepped out into the street. Then there was an explosion of light, and darkness again, as Frank and Joe crumpled under blows to their heads!

They awakened to the pungent smell of fish. How much time had passed neither boy knew. Joe looked up, glassy-eyed, into the face of Biff Hooper, who was bending over them.

"Take it easy," Biff said. "Just a bad bump on the noggin—both of you!"

Joe raised up on one elbow and winced. He had a splitting headache. Then he looked about. Both he and Frank were on a conveyor belt.

"Where—where are we?" asked Frank.

"In a fish factory. Don't you smell it?" Biff replied. "Right across the street from Rex Hall-bjornsson's."

"That faker!" Joe muttered. He swung into a sitting position and slid off the conveyor belt, rubbing his head gingerly.

Frank followed suit. "For Pete's sake," he said, "tell us what happened, Biff! How did we get here, and where did you come from?"

"Let's get out of here first, and I'll give you the whole story," Biff suggested. Walking the Hardys to their hotel, he explained that he had become worried about their trip to Akureyri. "I had a feeling you might be dry-gulched there. So I got a regular flight this morning and followed you."

"You must have left before our message arrived," Frank said. "When you didn't find us here, then what?"

Biff had gone to Hallbjornsson's address, but

he was not in. "The landlady told me the guy had come there only recently," he explained, "and she thought he was a foreigner."

Biff said he had wandered around town, watching the fishing boats and talking to American tourists. Then he had returned to Hallbjornsson's in the evening.

"I guess we arrived before you," Joe put in.

"Right. When I got here, I saw two men lurking in front of the house. I decided to play it by ear and stepped into an alley to see what would happen. A few minutes later you came out, and these fellows blackjacked you."

Frank gave a low whistle. "Now I know why Hallbjornsson got on the phone as soon as we came in!"

"Then," Biff continued, "a siren sounded, and you should have seen those fellows go to work. They dragged you into the fish factory. I was hoping it would be the police, but it was only an ambulance going past."

"So you followed the guys?" Joe asked.

Biff said that when the men did not come out of the building, he stole in to find the Hardys lying on the conveyor belt. "They must have scrammed out a side door," he concluded. "Now tell me, what happened to you?"

Frank gave him a brief report, and soon they reached the hotel. Frank and Joe got ice packs to apply to the lumps on their heads, and ordered a cot to be put in their room for Biff.

Next morning after breakfast the trio caught a plane back to Reykjavik. When their taxi arrived at the Saga Hotel, a strange sight greeted them. Chet was in front of the hotel, wandering about aimlessly.

"Hey, Chet!" Frank called out. The stout boy turned slowly and stood still. "Hi," he said listlessly.

"He sure looks funny," Frank stated. He said to Chet, "Come here!"

Chet obeyed, childlike.

Biff looked closely at him. "He isn't right. Look, Frank, his eyes are dilated."

Chet's head lolled as if he was in a stupor.

"I'll bet he's been drugged!" Joe cried out. "Holy toledo! Maybe somebody's upstairs fooling around with our radio and decoder!"

"Biff, take Chet to the front desk and get a doctor for him," Frank said quickly. "Joe and I will go upstairs."

The Hardys hastened into the hotel, dashed to an elevator, and let themselves out on their floor. Tiptoeing down the carpeted hall, they came to their room.

Someone was inside, moving about!

Frank silently inserted the key in the lock, turned it, and swung the door open.

Two men, taken by surprise, whirled around—the blond pilot and his phony rescuer!

CHAPTER IX

Man of the Sea

CAUGHT red-handed, the two men glared hatefully at the Hardys before diving for the door. Frank and Joe were bowled over and a furious melee ensued. Punching and cursing, the intruders bulled their way past the two boys.

Joe made a plunge for the blond man and got a firm grip on his wavy hair. But suddenly he was holding a wig in his hand! The thug was utterly bald!

Rex Hallbjornsson!

"Get him, Frank!"

The Hardys dashed along the hall, but the intruders made the elevator ahead of them.

"Down the stairway, Joe!"

The boys leaped three steps at a time in an effort to beat the elevator to the lobby. At the second floor the elevator doors opened. Out rushed the two men and raced down an adjacent corridor into a huge ballroom filled with tables and chairs.

Grabbing chairs as they ran, the thugs flung them into the path of the pursuers.

Frank hit one and fell flat. Joe stumbled over his brother. By the time they picked themselves up, the men had vanished down a back stairway and out of the building!

Disappointed, the Hardys limped upstairs. In Biff's room a doctor was examining Chet, a stethoscope to his ears.

"You say you had a cup of coffee with two strangers?" he asked as Frank and Joe walked in.

"That's right, Doc," replied Chet, who seemed much improved.

The Hardys introduced themselves, and the physician said, "Your friend will get over it all right. He was drugged. Do you have enemies?"

"Perhaps." Frank did not want to reveal their mission.

"Well, be careful. I am sorry such a thing had to happen to you in Iceland."

"Thanks for coming over so soon, Doc," said Biff. "What do we owe you?"

The doctor waved them off with a smile. "Nothing. Glad to help visitors." He put away his stethoscope and picked up his bag. "I would advise some exercise for you, young man. How about a swim in one of our warm water pools?"

"That'd be great!" Chet said, a big smile returning to his round face. "Where?"

"I suggest Sundholl. It is indoors, and not far from here."

The boys thanked the doctor again, and he left. Frank picked up the codebook from the safe, and they all went to the Hardys' room.

"Looks as if a cyclone hit it," Biff stated. "Are you sure one of them was Hallbjornsson?"

"No doubt about it," Joe replied. "First he looked for us at Keflavik Airport, then he followed us around the downtown area and finally kidnapped us in that plane."

"I feel kind of silly," Frank replied. "The blond wig and mustache disguise had us completely fooled."

The young detectives were relieved to find that the radio had not been damaged, nor had the intruders had time to locate the black box hidden in a corner of the clothes closet.

As Frank smoothed out two crumpled shirts, the telephone rang.

"Okay," he said. "Quiet, fellows. I have a hunch that these are our phony friends." Quickly he attached the recording device to the telephone and picked up the receiver. "Hello?" The boy made a wry face as he said, "Yes, sir. Thank you," and hung up.

"What was it?"

"The hotel manager. Asked us to cut down on the noise. Somebody complained."

Frank hit a chair and fell flat

They all laughed, and Chet quipped, "Sure, we'll be quiet, if the crooks promise, too."

The phone rang again, and this time Joe scooped it up. The voice on the other end was harsh. "Hardys, get out of Iceland!" This was followed by heavy breathing into the mouthpiece, then the caller hung up.

"Why—those dirty bums!" Joe said hotly. "They're trying to scare us out of this country!"

"Fat chance!" Chet said bravely.

"Did you recognize the voice?" asked Biff.

"The phony Hallbjornsson! Who else?"

With the room set to rights again, the four boys had lunch, then sprawled on the beds and the two chairs, trying to find a logical answer to all that had happened.

Why did the phony Hallbjornsson want to kidnap Frank and Joe? Obviously he had impersonated Hallbjornsson only for that purpose. Who was he really?

Finally Chet Morton stood up and stretched. "Well, Frank and Joe, you're the brains department. Try to figure it out while Biff and I go for a warm water swim!"

"I'm for it!" said Biff.

"You can get the address at the desk," Joe advised. "Call a taxi, but be careful about drinking coffee with strangers!"

A few minutes later there was a light tap on

the Hardys' door. Frank opened it. Gummi stood outside.

"Come on in," Frank invited. "What's new?"

"Plenty!" Gummi took a chair, wet his lips, and settled back with a great air of satisfaction. "I've been busy with some detective work to help you."

"Any luck so far?" Joe asked.

"I'll say! I tried to get in touch with you yesterday, but you were always out. I've found your man Rex!"

"No kidding!"

Gummi leaned forward and gestured with his hands. "Now, I won't guarantee that this is the guy you really want. He's an old seaman who's out on a fishing trawler called the *Svartfugel*—it means blackbird."

"How do we get in touch with him?" Frank asked.

Gummi explained that the trawler was at sea but that he had found out where the *Svartfugel*'s skipper lived. "His name is Rensson. Perhaps his wife can tell us something about this Rex," he added.

"What are we waiting for? Let's scram!" Joe said excitedly. They hastened down to the lobby, hopped into Gummi's jeep, and drove to a neat yellow house near the waterfront.

Gummi knocked, and a tall blond woman answered. The youth questioned her in Icelandic. "*Ja, ja,*" she replied. "Rex Mar."

"*Tack, tack,*" Gummi said and continued the interrogation. After they had left, Frank said, "What's the pitch, Gummi?"

The boy explained that Rex's name was Mar.

"Like the sea?" Joe recognized the word.

"Right. Rex is supposed to be an old salt, and full of sea stories."

"And where is he now?" Frank questioned.

"Somewhere off the northwest coast."

"We can't overlook any possible clue," Joe mused. "Maybe he changed his last name because it was too long." The boys had learned from their detective father that even the slightest clue can sometimes solve a difficult case.

Gummi dropped the boys off at the hotel and said good-by. He would see them later.

Frank checked the desk for any messages. There were none. Then he and Joe went up to their room.

"I'm really getting worried," Frank said. "Joe, I think we ought to contact Dad and tell him what happened." He unlimbered the radio and began to send out signals. As he did, someone pounded on the door.

"Good night!" Joe jumped up. "What's going on?" He opened the door.

Chet Morton burst in, his face flushed with excitement. "Guess who we met?"

"We can't guess!" Frank said.

"Come with me—downstairs—now!"

"Chet, have you gone wacky?" Joe asked.

Frank turned off the radio, and the Hardys followed their friend. When they stepped into the elevator, Frank tried to question his excited buddy. "Did you catch the phony Hallbjornsson?"

"You'll see!"

A few seconds later they arrived in the lobby. There was Biff Hooper chatting gaily with Steina the stewardess!

CHAPTER X

The Arctic Patrol

"HELLO, Steina. How are you?" Frank said, extending a hand to the smiling black-haired girl.

Joe, meanwhile, glanced about the lobby. "Chet, I thought you found Hallbjornsson."

"No, it was Steina we found, and guess where— at the swimming pool!"

"I was glad to meet them on my day off," said Steina. Then she turned to Chet with a wink. "Tell me, have you found any Eskimos yet?"

"No, but we've had our adventures," the stout boy replied. But this time he kept his secrets to himself. They moved to the side of the lobby and took comfortable seats around a coffee table.

Biff Hooper spoke to Frank in a low voice. "Do you think Steina might be able to help us? She probably knows lots of important people in Iceland."

"Yes, she might," Frank replied and looked at the stewardess. "Steina, we'd like to contact a man named Rex Mar on the fishing trawler *Svartfugel*. Do you know how we can get in touch with him?"

"Of course," the girl answered with a wave of her hand, as if the request were an easy one.

Joe had his doubts. "You're not kidding, are you?"

"No. My uncle Oscar will help you, I'm sure."

"Your uncle Oscar?" Chet raised his eyebrows. "Who's he?"

"Head of the Icelandic coast guard," Steina replied, cocking her head coyly.

"Great!" Joe exclaimed. "Will you give us an introduction?"

Without a word the girl rose, went to a wall telephone nearby, and dialed a number. After chatting in Icelandic, she hung up and returned to the boys. "Uncle Oscar Sigtryggsson is in his office. He's expecting you."

"Thanks a million, Steina," Frank said. "Can we see him in half an hour?"

"Sure. I must be going along now," the girl replied. Waving good-by, she left in her small car which she had parked in front of the hotel.

The boys went directly to the Hardys' room, where Frank and Joe clued their buddies in on the Mar information. Then Joe flicked on their radio and began sending signals. Fifteen minutes later they received an answer. The conversation was amiable and casual. Frank told his father that the only Hallbjornsson they had found so far proved to be the wrong one, but that they had had some trouble getting rid of him.

Afterward, Joe rapidly figured out their father's message. Mr. Hardy said that the high Icelandic officials now knew that his sons were working on the astronaut case. He also warned them to beware of a Felix Musselman.

The description of this man fit the phony Hallbjornsson to a T. Originally a Rumanian, Musselman had fake passports for several countries. "He may be tied in with the astronaut case. Exercise extreme caution!" Mr. Hardy ended.

Frank returned the radio to the hiding place in the closet.

"Wow!" Joe said. "So Hallbjornsson-Musselman may be an agent of a spy network mixed up in the astronaut case!"

"That's probably his primary mission," Frank reasoned. "When he found out we were coming to Iceland, his second mission was capturing us in order to get us out of the way. He must have been afraid we would get involved with the case."

"Now what?" Biff asked.

"Well, we'd better go see Steina's uncle. You and Chet stay here and stand guard. Okay?"

Soon Frank and Joe arrived at the Icelandic coast guard headquarters, called by the almost unpronounceable name of Landhelgisgaezlan. Its offices were located on Seljaveg, close to the waterfront.

"The Hardy boys?" a male clerk asked as they entered.

"Right. Frank and Joe, from Bayport, U.S.A."

"Captain Sigtryggsson is waiting for you. This way, please."

He ushered the visitors into an office with nautical decorations and closed the door. They were greeted by a tall gray-haired man who rose from his chair behind a long desk.

"So," he said, after shaking hands and offering the boys two chairs, "you are American detectives!"

"Yes," said Joe. "I know we're still young, but—"

"Not at all," the captain replied. "Our best men in the coast guard are young fellows like you. We start them at fifteen, and by the time they are eighteen or nineteen, believe me, they are excellent seamen. Your father is a world-famous detective and I gather he has trained you well in his profession."

Frank and Joe felt much at home in the presence of Captain Sigtryggsson. "You have a very fine niece in Steina," said Frank, returning the compliment.

"That's what the boys tell me," the captain

said with a smile. *"Ja, ja.* Now tell me, what is your question?"

"We wish to speak to a man named Rex Hall-bjornsson," Frank began. "He may be Rex Mar, sailing on the trawler *Svartfugel.*"

"I think I can help you," the captain said. He rose from his chair and went to a map hanging on the wall. "The *Svartfugel* is probably fishing in waters near Snaefellsjokull."

"The glacier?" asked Joe.

"Ja. Right here. Perhaps ten miles offshore. We will send you up there."

The boys were thunderstruck. "Really?" asked Joe. "How?"

"On the *Thor.* Are you good seamen?"

"Pretty good," Frank replied.

The Icelander walked over to the model of a ship sitting on a table beside the boys.

"This is the *Thor,*" he explained. "You know, we don't have a large navy, but it is a good one." He said that the *Thor* was setting out the next day on a fourteen-day tour of duty in Icelandic waters.

"Your Arctic Patrol—isn't that what you call it?" Frank remarked.

The captain nodded and continued. "Naturally, I don't think it will take fourteen days to find the *Svartfugel.*"

"Then how'll we get back?" Joe asked.

"We'll arrange that later. Perhaps on the

Albert. It is a smaller boat on its way back to Keflavik from a two-week tour." The captain sat down at his desk again and looked straight at the boys. "You are working on the McGeorge case, too!"

Frank and Joe were startled. "Yes. It's top secret," Frank managed to reply.

"Of course. It is most unusual to have civilians involved. But perhaps you can be of help."

"We already have a clue," Frank said, and told about the leather glove. "It matches a similar one we got at the base in Keflavik." He explained how they had found it, and when.

"Excellent. But Major McGeorge disappeared earlier than that. We searched the area of the sulfur pit."

"Perhaps he came back," Frank offered. "Maybe his captors threatened to throw him in if he didn't tell his NASA secrets."

"A good possibility," the captain admitted. "We'll look into this."

The boys rose and thanked him, promising to be at his office at two o'clock the next afternoon.

"Captain Carl Magnusson, the skipper of the *Thor*, will be here to meet you," their host said as he ushered the Hardys to the door.

When they returned to their hotel, they found Chet and Biff brimming with excitement. "Here's another letter answering your ad in the paper," Biff said.

Frank opened it. A Hallbjornsson living in Hafnarfjordur thought that he might be a relative of the man called Rex.

Frank shook his head. "Now we've got two leads to follow."

"What did the coast guard chief have to say?"

"We're leaving on one of their boats tomorrow."

"That was fast. Well, suppose Chet and I go down to Hafnarfjordur and investigate the other guy?"

"Great idea!"

Chet and Biff departed the next morning, and at two o'clock the Hardys, traveling as lightly as they could, appeared at Captain Sigtryggsson's office.

There they met a tall, handsome man in his late thirties—Carl Magnusson, the skipper of the *Thor*. After hard handshakes, Captain Magnusson said, "Come with me, men. We're on our way."

He took them down the harbor where the *Thor*, a spotless white cutter, was waiting.

"She's a big ship," Frank observed.

"Two hundred and six feet long—nine hundred and twenty tons," the captain explained.

As they stepped from the dock down a ladder to board the cutter, Frank and Joe noticed a 57 mm gun mounted on the front of the boat. Behind the gun deck, at a lower level, lay a large rubber raft. Two pontoons on either side were bullet-shaped.

"We use that for transfers in rough weather," said Captain Magnusson, who had noticed the boys' inquisitive looks.

They followed the skipper up and down a maze of companionways to his quarters. A comfortable wardroom was located forward, and the captain's bunk was to the left. On the right side were quarters for the visitors.

"Make yourselves at home," Captain Magnusson said.

"Do you suppose you can find the *Svartfugel* for us?" Joe asked, putting down his bag.

"I think so, if we don't run into any foreign poachers." The skipper explained that recently some ships of foreign registry had been sneaking through the twelve-mile limit. "But we spot them on radar," he continued, "and get them!"

"Then what do you do?" Frank asked.

"Bring them back to port and fine them. They cannot get away with our codfish!"

Frank and Joe looked about the ship. Several seamen, about their own age, were busy hosing and swabbing the decks. Some of them spoke English, and the boys chatted with them about their training and their ambitions.

Then they strolled about, looking at the colorful Icelandic coastline slipping past.

"You know," Joe said to his brother, "I'm beginning to enjoy our trip!"

"Well, let's hope we're successful," Frank replied with a grin.

About sundown, Snaefell Glacier came into view, its bare, rugged peaks bathed in orange light. Suddenly Captain Magnusson, who stood on the bridge, beckoned to the Hardys. They hastened up a ladder and were at his side a moment later.

"Look over there!" the skipper said tersely, peering through his binoculars. "A poacher! She's in our territorial waters!"

He handed Frank the binoculars, so high-powered that they brought the fishing trawler seemingly close enough to touch. She was about forty-five feet long and bore the name *Tek*.

Frank surveyed her from stem to stern. Five crewmen could be seen on deck. Suddenly he gasped. "Joe, there he is!"

"Who?"

"Musselman. I'll bet anything!"

CHAPTER XI

Over the Waves

Joe took the glasses to confirm Frank's suspicion. No doubt about it! The face was that of the bogus Hallbjornsson!

"Captain Magnusson," Frank said, "there's a wanted man on the *Tek*!"

"The entire trawler is wanted," the captain replied with a grim smile. "She's poaching in Icelandic waters."

He dispatched a radio message commanding the *Tek* to stop. Then he took the binoculars and watched. Suddenly he gave an exclamation in Icelandic. The trawler was turning about and racing toward the open sea!

"She's trying to get away!" Frank cried out.

If Captain Magnusson was startled by the poacher's action, he did not show it. Calmly he gave the order for full speed ahead.

Much to the surprise of Frank and Joe, the fleeing boat had exceptional speed. Churning up a greenish-white wake, it high-tailed straight west. But it was no match for the *Thor*. The cutter gained with every minute.

Finally the ships came side by side. Captain Magnusson, using a bullhorn, ordered the fleeing boat to stop for boarding. "You are under arrest!" he thundered.

Beckoning to the Hardy boys and two seamen, he boarded the poacher and was met by her irate skipper, who declared in broken English, "You cannot stop us. It is illegal!"

"You are in Icelandic fishing waters," Captain Magnusson replied evenly. "And you are not Icelandic."

"I am thirteen miles off your shore!"

"Only ten by my calculations. And my calculations are what count." Magnussen asked curtly, "Why did you flee when I radioed for you to stop?"

"I did not hear your message."

"Then you should get your radio repaired. What you did was dangerous; you could have been shot."

The captain accompanied the poacher to his bridge, where he obtained the fishing boat's registration and other vital details. Then Magnusson said, "I think you are harboring a fugitive from Iceland and will conduct a search."

The poacher glared at him in rage. "How dare you! You cannot do this!"

"But we will," Magnussen retorted. He motioned to Frank and Joe, along with his two crewmen. The four conducted a painstaking search for the fugitive, expecting to see Musselman pop out of a closet or jump out of a locker at any moment. But the baldheaded spy could not be found.

"Maybe he's hiding in some kind of a container," Frank said.

"You mean under the boat?" Joe asked.

"It's possible."

Although they searched the sides of the boat for any telltale line leading under the water, their efforts were fruitless.

"Come on. We'll give the crew's quarters one more look," Frank said.

The bunks were thoroughly checked to see if anyone was hiding under a false mattress. Each mattress was thumped, but all were genuine. No Musselman!

The crewmen left. Frank and Joe gave the last bunk one more look. A small bit of paper stuck between the wall and the blanket caught Frank's eye. He plucked it from its hiding place.

"Holy crow! Joe, look at this!" It had been torn from an Icelandic newspaper.

"It's our ad!" Joe exclaimed. "The one Musselman answered!"

"See, we were right!" Frank said. "He was on this boat!"

"One thing is sure," Joe muttered. "That crook isn't here now, and if he is, he certainly is well hidden."

The boys decided not to tell Captain Magnusson about their clue. When they returned to the bridge, the skipper asked, "Any luck?"

"No. We couldn't find him." Frank observed the poaching captain all the while. He did not twitch a muscle, and his eyes remained cold and angry. If he knew of Musselman's presence, he gave no indication.

Magnusson called for his first lieutenant, who vaulted over the rail.

"Hjalmar, take this boat to Reykjavik. We will follow!"

After admonishing his prisoners not to do anything rash, Magnusson returned to the *Thor,* with the Hardys at his heels. The coast guard cutter and its captive turned about and were under way toward the Icelandic capital city.

In the captain's cabin Frank and Joe talked with the skipper. "What'll happen to these fellows now?" Frank asked.

"They will be fined, and their fish confiscated."

"But what about our search for Rex Mar?" Joe asked.

A broad smile came over the captain's face. "I

knew you would ask that question. Everything has been taken care of."

"How?"

"We will pass the *Albert* about two o'clock this morning. We will transfer you for the continuation of your search for Rex Mar."

"Great!" Frank said. "Thank you, sir."

"But it will not be as easy as boarding the poacher," the skipper went on. "You see how rough it is getting? We will have to transfer you by raft."

The *Thor* had begun to pitch and yaw. As night settled over the sea, the wind blew harder.

"We may be in for a little rough weather," the captain declared. "But you are good sailors, right?"

Joe hoped that neither of them would get seasick. But he felt a little queasy already. Dinner with the crew, however, settled Joe's stomach. The boys joined the young crewmen in a hearty meal of roast lamb and boiled potatoes. The coffee was black and piping hot.

When they returned to the deck again, the swell was even greater, and the ship rolled and rocked.

"Get some sleep now," the captain advised them. "We will wake you when the *Albert* comes in sight."

Frank and Joe slipped into their bunks and

the rolling sea lolled them to sleep in no time at all. The next thing Frank knew, there was a hand on his shoulder.

"Come. We have the *Albert* in sight," Captain Magnusson said. "You have your gear ready?"

"Yes, we're all packed," Frank replied as Joe rose sleepily from his bunk.

On deck the fresh wind with the bite of glacier snow assailed the Hardys' nostrils, and they were instantly wide awake.

In the distance the lights of the *Albert* bobbed up and down. Captain Magnusson gave an order, and a searchlight atop the mast shone down on the sea in a brilliant yellow cone.

"There comes the raft now," the skipper said, pointing over the sea. At first it looked like a cork; then, as it drew closer, Frank and Joe saw that it was identical to the one lashed on the forward deck of the *Thor*. Three seamen, using long oars as paddles, propelled the raft toward them.

On the *Thor* a section of rail was lifted up, and as the raft drew alongside, one of the sailors hurled a line aboard.

"Everything is perfectly safe," Captain Magnusson assured the boys.

Frank wondered. The raft rose and fell on each wave, coming even with the deck of the *Thor*, then dropping ten feet into the trough.

Clutching their bags, the Hardys waited. Up

came the raft. Joe stepped in, and went down like an elevator. Up it came again for Frank. Then the line was cast off, and they were gliding over the frigid sea.

The raft resembled a small bug struggling in the rolling waves. Overhead, a silver moon illuminated the snow-capped mountains along the shore.

The young seamen paddled hard. Their oars flashed as they dug deep into the brine.

Frank's eyes scanned the ocean. Suddenly he leaned over to Joe. "Something else is out there!"

"Where?" asked Joe, looking about in the stiff breeze.

"I saw a wake!"

Joe peered intently, but could spot nothing. "What do you suppose it was?"

"A small boat, or a raft, maybe with a motor!"

Presently the *Albert* loomed up black beside the raft. A section of its deck rail also had been lifted, but Frank Hardy was not ready to board yet. Crouched in the raft, he looked up at the captain and shouted, "I think I saw another small boat out there, skipper. I'd like permission to look for it!"

"What? Speak slower, please. I am not too good with English."

Frank repeated his request, and the captain called back, "Wait. I will try first to find it on my radar." He went into the control room, while the raft, banging against the side of the *Albert,* rose and fell with a dizzying motion.

The seamen did their best to hold everything steady, and two more aboard the *Albert* clung to the line which had been thrown to them.

Then suddenly it happened. A huge wave bore down on them. It hit the raft while it was in a deep trough, and after it had passed over the clinging occupants, Frank Hardy was gone!

CHAPTER XII

A Mysterious Offer

A HEAD bobbed to the surface beside the *Albert,* then disappeared beneath the sullen waves again. Instantly two of the crewmen sprang overboard, while the third restrained Joe from diving in after his brother.

Someone on the deck flashed a powerful light on the turbulent waters and Joe saw Frank in the firm grasp of the two seamen. His face was pale, his eyes shut.

Frank was pushed into the raft, then hoisted quickly to the deck of the *Albert.* Seconds later, on a rising wave, Joe stepped safely aboard.

The *Albert's* captain, a square-jawed man named Holmquist, immediately applied artificial respiration to Frank, and finally the boy's eyes fluttered open. The captain helped him to his feet. "You tried to swallow all of the North Atlantic, but it cannot be done!"

"I sure did go under, like a sinker," Frank said, shivering from the icy water.

"Come down below and change into some dry clothes," Captain Holmquist said.

Still groggy, Frank followed him and Joe into a warm cabin. There he was supplied with seamen's clothes, while his own were hung up to dry. Then the three sat down at the table in the skipper's quarters.

"Did you see the other raft?" was Joe's first question.

"Something was out there," said Captain Holmquist. "But a raft—I doubt that. Probably a whale. We have them in these waters, you know."

"We can't look for it any more, then?" Frank asked.

The skipper shrugged. "There's nothing on our radar now. Anyhow, our mission is to find the *Svartfugel*, right?"

"That's what we came for." Frank managed a grin. "You think you can find her?"

"I found her already. She is located on our chart. In the morning you will have your trawler served up for breakfast!"

Frank and Joe laughed at the captain's good humor and thanked him again for his help. Then they retired to their bunks and fell fast asleep.

The *Albert* was alive with the sound of ship's noises when the Hardys awakened. Footsteps sounded on gangways, and the smell of ham and hot coffee drifted into their cabin.

By this time Frank's clothes had dried. The boys dressed hurriedly and found their way to the breakfast table. The seamen joked about Frank's dunking.

"He went down like a seal!" said one of his rescuers with a chuckle.

"More like a walrus I would say," Frank replied, and took his place at the square table beside Captain Holmquist.

"Now you will have something to tell back home," the skipper said.

The Hardys had soft-boiled eggs, cereal, and milk. In the center of the table stood a tall can of cod-liver oil. After watching the seamen help themselves, Frank and Joe each took a large spoonful, washed down by a second glass of milk.

"Now you're all set for the *Svartfugel*," Captain Holmquist said. "She's off our port bow, if you'd like to take a look."

The boys hastened to the deck and looked across the leaden waters toward a tubby little trawler. The captain followed with his bullhorn. In Icelandic he asked if Rex Mar was aboard.

"*Ja, ja,*" came the answer.

The ocean was calm enough for the two boats to pull alongside and soon Frank and Joe dropped to the deck of the *Svartfugel*.

"Take your time," Captain Holmquist said. "We will wait for you."

The small boat had only a crew of five, and its skipper called below decks for Rex Mar. The man appeared, wearing a brown sweater. Its turtleneck set off a square, weather-beaten face, topped by a patch of flowing gray hair beneath a seaman's cap.

Frank Hardy extended a hand in greeting. Rex Mar's looked like a bear paw in comparison.

"I'm Frank Hardy. Do you speak English, Mr. Mar?"

"Yes."

Joe introduced himself and said, "There's something we would like you to do."

"No, I won't do it!" Mar said and turned down the narrow gangway.

"Wait a minute!" Frank called out. "You won't do what?"

The old fellow regarded them grimly through watery blue eyes. "I won't do what you want me to do. I was asked before. The answer is still No!"

Frank and Joe exchanged puzzled glances. Finally Frank said, "Mr. Mar, we only want you to identify yourself."

Rex Mar closed one eye suspiciously. "Rex Mar is the name, and that's all."

From the rail of the *Albert,* Holmquist looked down with a slight smile of amusement on his face. In rapid-fire Icelandic he spoke with the old seaman. Instantly Mar seemed more ready to cooperate.

"What is it you want to know?"

"We are looking for Rex Hallbjornsson," Frank said.

"Why?"

"Somebody left him some insurance money."

The man's face lit up like the aurora borealis. "Rex Hallbjornsson. *Ja,* I am the one!"

Frank and Joe beamed at each other and shook hands vigorously. "Frank, we've done it!" said Joe. "We found our man!"

But the elder Hardy boy was not convinced that the man standing before them was the real Rex Hallbjornsson.

"Tell us," he said, "how, why, and when did you change your name?"

The old seaman took a pail, turned it upside down, and used it for a seat. Frank and Joe leaned against the capstan and listened to his tale.

Mar said that he once was shipwrecked off the coast of France. After he had been rescued, his name Hallbjornsson—hard to spell for foreigners —had been recorded incorrectly.

"I went to Spain," he said, "where my name was spelled wrong again. What a mess it was! The *b, j,* and the *l*'s were all mixed up. I don't think anybody could sneeze the name!"

Joe chuckled at the description. "So you changed it?"

"Yes. I chose the name Mar because it means sea. You see, I had to do it. In Spain they thought I was a spy since all the names on my papers were spelled differently. And you know," he said, rubbing the side of his nose, "somebody still thinks I'm a spy."

"Who?" asked Frank.

"Two men. They came to see me."

"About what?" Joe wanted to know.

"About a job." Mar explained that someone wanted the help of a man who knew the coast of Iceland intimately. "But I didn't take it!"

The Hardys were immediately alerted by the strange request. Frank said, "If they ever come to you with that proposal again, will you let me know?"

"All right," Mar replied, glancing up at Captain Holmquist.

Convinced that Mar was indeed Rex Hallbjornsson, Frank told him that he had been named the beneficiary in a life insurance policy paying fifty thousand dollars. The old fellow's jaw dropped, and he stood up, looking bewildered.

When the name of the policyholder was given, a faraway look came into his eyes. He told the Hardys that it was a man he saved from drowning. "Now he will make my old age a comfortable one," Mar said with feeling.

Frank suggested that he come with them, leaving the trawler at once. "You'll have to sign some papers in Reykjavik, and then we'll try to get your money as soon as possible, Mr. Mar."

The *Svartfugel's* skipper gave permission for his crewman to leave, and Rex Mar and the boys boarded the *Albert.*

It was late in the afternoon when the coast guard boat pulled into Reykjavik Harbor. The Hardys thanked Captain Holmquist and his crew, then stepped onto the dock. The old seaman followed. A taxi took them into town. Mar was let off at his rooming house, with instructions to await word from the boys, and Frank and Joe continued on to their hotel.

After hastening upstairs, they rapped on the door of Chet's room. No answer. They went to their own room and phoned the desk. Had Biff and Chet left any message?

The answer nearly floored them. Their friends had checked out of the hotel the day before.

"What's going on?" Frank asked the clerk.

The man did not know, except that he had observed the pair talking with Gummi shortly before they signed out.

Instantly Joe got on the phone to their Icelandic friend. "Gummi, where are Chet and Biff?"

"You should know! They left after getting your message!"

CHAPTER XIII

Eavesdroppers

"WE didn't send any message!" Joe exclaimed, holding the receiver so that Frank could follow the conversation.

"Oh no!" Gummi said that Chet and Biff had returned from an unsuccessful visit to Hafnarfjordur and shortly afterward received word ostensibly from Frank and Joe to meet them somewhere.

"Good night! That was a hoax! Tell me, where were they to meet us?"

"They didn't say. Chet only told me it was a secret."

The Hardys were worried. Obviously this was an attempt by Musselman to split the ranks and deal with them individually.

Frank took the phone from Joe. "If we only had a clue! A single clue! Think hard, Gummi. Didn't Chet or Biff drop some kind of hint where they were going?"

"Yes, Chet did," Gummi said after a thoughtful pause. "He mentioned that he had better get some seasick pills."

"That's all?"

"Yes."

"Well, if you remember anything else, Gummi, give us a ring, will you?"

"Sure thing."

Frank hung up.

"At least we know they were going somewhere by boat," Joe said.

"Don't jump to conclusions, Joe. The deduction might be true, and it might not."

"If it were," Joe reasoned, "perhaps Chet and Biff went somewhere off the coast of Snaefell Glacier where you saw the mysterious raft!"

"There's only one thing to do now—inform the police and the coast guard," Frank said crisply. "I'll call them right away."

After he had notified the authorities about their missing friends, Frank telephoned Captain Magnusson. The skipper told him that the poachers had been heavily fined. The *Tek* was also fine-combed again, but the only thing found was a coil of fine nylon line attached to an underwater hook. No sign of a man fitting the description of Musselman.

Then Frank told the captain about Chet and Biff.

"The *Thor* is going on patrol again tonight,

Frank," Magnusson said. "If they are anywhere in the Icelandic waters, we'll find them!"

"Thanks, Captain." Frank hung up and turned to Joe. Quickly he told him the news. "Obviously the nylon line was for towing something," he concluded.

"Yes, but we didn't see any boat behind the *Tek*," replied Joe.

"I know. It's a puzzler all right."

"What's next?"

"Let's have something to eat, then we'll radio Dad."

After a quick supper the boys contacted their father. They got through to Texas immediately.

Frank reported that they had found Rex Mar, and Mr. Hardy congratulated them. Then he spelled out in detail an affidavit, which Frank was to prepare for the man to sign. The boy copied down the document, then told about Chet and Biff's mysterious disappearance.

Mr. Hardy expressed his worry, and casually switched to code. He was sure that the boys' disappearance was tied in with the astronaut case.

"If you find Musselman, you will probably find Biff and Chet," Mr. Hardy advised.

After their father signed off, the boys tried to map out a plan of action.

"We're really stuck," Joe muttered. "The only clue is that Chet and Biff may be on a boat, and we can't chase them on the ocean."

"The coast guard'll have to do it," Frank admitted. "But where to find Musselman? As far as he's concerned, we don't have any clues at all!"

Joe sighed. "How about going over to Rex Mar with the affidavit? There's not much else we can do tonight."

"Okay."

The boys walked the short distance to the sailor's place. He occupied a large room on the first floor.

Mar greeted them cordially, putting down his pipe on a small table to shake hands with them. He offered them chairs, then sank back onto a sofa and sent ringlets of smoke from his pipe.

"You look pretty happy, Mr. Mar," Frank said jovially.

"I am a rich man."

"You will be, after a few formalities," Joe agreed as Frank produced the affidavit.

Rex Mar held it at arm's length, scrutinizing every word, then he took the pen proffered by Frank in his gnarled fingers and scratched his name at the bottom of the paper.

"After this is processed in the States," Frank said, "you will receive your money."

"Fine," Mar replied. Then he looked at the Hardys seriously. "I have something to tell you," he said as Frank returned the affidavit to his pocket. "They were here again to see me."

"Who was?"

"The men who think I am a spy. You asked me to tell you."

"Thanks for the tip," Frank replied, leaning forward in his chair. "What did they say?"

"They want me to get a boat and help them take something out of the country illegally!"

"What did you tell them?"

"I said I wanted to think it over. They will return in an hour for my answer. I was about to call you when you rang my bell."

"Mr. Mar, what did these fellows look like?" Joe queried.

"One was bald, short, and heavy-set. The other was black-haired with a rather long nose. They are due here any minute."

Frank and Joe exchanged glances. There was no doubt in their minds that the men were Musselman and his pal.

"What do you want me to do?" Mar asked.

"Go along with their proposition," Frank said.

"But it is illegal!"

"That's just it. We might be able to uncover a nefarious scheme."

"All right. I will do as you say. You go now and I'll tell you later exactly what they want me to do."

Joe looked around. "I have a better idea. We'll listen in." He pointed to a small closet. "Can we both get in there?"

Mar sucked on his pipe, sending out a billow of smoke. "I think so."

He opened the closet, which was rank with the odor of old clothes. A few tools were stacked in one corner. The boys squeezed in. A narrow crack between the floor and the bottom of the door would allow enough air to keep them from suffocating.

"When they come, I will get them to leave as soon as possible," Rex Mar said.

Frank coughed a bit, and Joe's throat burned, as he inhaled the pipe smoke which drifted over the room like an early-morning heavy fog.

The doorbell rang. As Mar went to answer it, Frank and Joe ducked into the closet. Seconds later they heard Mar return with a visitor. The voice was unmistakable. *Musselman!*

Frank and Joe hardly dared to breathe, lest any sound give away their eavesdropping hideout.

"All right now," said Mar. "Tell me just what do you want me to do?"

"How many times must I tell you?" the caller replied impatiently. "I want you to rent a small fishing boat."

"And then what?"

"Are you absolutely daft, old man?" snapped Musselman. "Go to the coast near Snaefellsjokull and I'll be waiting for you there. Look, here's the spot."

Frank and Joe heard the crinkling of paper as a map was spread out on the table.

"Yes. I see it," said Mar. "But I cannot sail such a boat all alone."

"Then get yourself a crew. I will pay you well."

"How many will you pay for?"

"Three good men. It may be a rough trip."

Joe could not resist whispering to his brother. Putting his lips close to Frank's ear, he said, "Let's turn the tables on this goon! We'll go with Mar, and at the same time we can hunt for Biff and Chet!"

There came the scraping sound of chairs pushed back from the table as the caller prepared to leave.

"I'm leaving Reykjavik early tomorrow morning," Musselman said, then added, "I can trust you to take care of this assignment?"

"Ja."

"Then here is an advance payment. Get a seaworthy boat and do it as quickly as possible."

Joe longed for the man to depart. The stuffy air in the closet and the tobacco smoke filled his lungs. How good it would be to inhale some fresh air!

"Good-by," Mar said, and the boys heard the door close. But before they could open the closet, the lock clicked shut.

Frank tried to turn the knob and stifled a gasp. They were trapped!

Frank and Joe ducked into the closet

CHAPTER XIV

A Perfect Disguise

"JOE, we're locked in!"

"Holy crow! Were we ever suckered by Rex Mar! Frank, what are we going to do?"

The boys talked in hushed whispers.

"Let's not panic. We'll get out. Easy does it, Joe."

"Yes. But suppose they're out there waiting for us?"

"That's the chance we'll have to take," Frank replied, feeling about the dark closet.

"What are you looking for?" Joe asked.

His brother said that he had seen some tools. Maybe one of them would be of use. By this time it had become insufferably hot. Perspiration began to drip from their faces.

"If we had only carried a flashlight!" Joe muttered. He pressed his ear close to the door. There **was no** sound outside. If Mar was in league with the criminals, perhaps he had left with Mussel-man.

"Joe, I found something!"

"What is it?"

"A jack."

"Good. Now if we had a two-by-four—" With both hands Joe rummaged the floor of the closet. "Here's something—a block of wood!"

"How long?"

"Not long enough."

Frank's hand touched a large hammer. "Now I think we have it, Joe!"

Pushing the old clothes to one side, he placed the base of the jack against the rear wall of the closet. Joe held the block of wood and the hammer end to end between the door and the head of the jack. They fit loosely.

Using an old wrench handle, Frank activated the jack. *Click! Click! Click!* Their improvised battering ram was wedged tightly between the back of the closet and the door. Frank applied more pressure. The door creaked a little. Could their device spring the lock?

Click! Click! Crash! The lock was forced and the door sprang open.

The room was not empty after all. There sat Rex Mar, puffing on his pipe and smiling.

Slack-jawed, Frank and Joe looked at him in amazement. "What—what—? Why did you do that?" Frank asked.

Joe's fists were clenched in anger. "You nearly suffocated us. Is this your idea of fun?"

The old sailor motioned the boys to simmer down. "You proved yourselves," he said. "I wanted to see what you would do in a difficult situation."

"Then you knew the jack was in the closet?" Frank asked.

Mar nodded. He went to the refrigerator and pulled out a bottle of cold water. Frank and Joe each gulped down a glassful.

Now calm after their ordeal, Frank asked, "Was that the blond man you spoke to?"

"Right. Did you see him through the keyhole?"

"How could we! The key was in it," Joe said caustically.

"Yes. I forgot."

"What was his name?"

"He did not tell me."

"How about your crew?" Frank went on.

"You two, of course," Mar replied. "I told you, you proved yourselves."

Frank and Joe nodded to each other. They would have to level with Mar.

"We'll need disguises," Frank said.

"What for?" The old seaman looked surprised.

"Judging from the voice of your visitor, he might be a member of a gang we're after. We'll get the third crewman, too, an Icelandic friend of ours by the name of Gudmundur. You can depend on him."

"Good." Mar asked no further questions. "I will look for a suitable boat. When I find one, I will call you at your hotel."

The boys agreed and bid the seaman good-by. Even though it was very late, they stopped at police headquarters to find out if any word had been received about the missing Biff and Chet. The report was negative.

Glum and disappointed, Frank and Joe returned to the Saga Hotel. They sat quietly in their room for a while, mulling over the entire situation.

"I must confess," Frank said, "that I'm still not thoroughly convinced about Rex Mar."

"I know," Joe said. "We're putting ourselves in his hands. If he turns out to be one of Mussel-man's guys, we're really in for it."

"On the other hand, if he's in league with Musselman, why did he tell us about this 'illegal' job to begin with? Why did he let us know that he knew Musselman, and why did he let us overhear their conversation?"

"Search me."

"Well, with Gummi it'll be three against one on that trawler. I think we can handle the situation."

A phone call brought the Icelandic boy to the

hotel early the next morning. "Any word from Biff and Chet yet?" he asked as he came in the door.

"No. But it seems we found the right Hallbjornsson."

"Great! Now your official mission is over, and once you find Chet and Biff you can have some fun in Iceland."

"Well, there's a complication," Joe replied, "The fake Hallbjornsson is trying to get the real Hallbjornsson involved in a smuggling job and—"

Gummi interrupted the boy with a gesture of his hand. "Now look, fellows! You gave me that story about being detectives on an insurance case, and I bought it. Now you're overdoing it. I'm not exactly stupid, you know. Either you level with me, or I'll exit right here and now!"

"Calm down, Gummi," Frank said. "We are American detectives on an insurance case, and everything we told you is true. But we got involved in something else—" He exchanged a quick glance with Joe, who nodded his agreement.

"Well?" Gummi still had a suspicious look on his face.

"Will you promise to keep it to yourself? It's a top-secret affair concerning both the American and the Icelandic governments.

"I'll keep quiet."

Frank and Joe revealed everything to their

friend. When the Icelander heard the story, he eagerly pledged his support as a crewman.

"I might be able to help my country, too," he said enthusiastically. "Are you going to tell the coast guard?"

"Yes. I'll phone Captain Sigtryggsson and clue him in on our plans. He knows we are working on the case," Frank said.

"When do we start?" Gummi asked.

"As soon as Rex Mar finds a boat," Joe replied.

"And you and I will have to work up disguises," Frank put in. "We'll go down to the barbershop right now and have our hair dyed. Gummi, can you get us some old seamen's clothes?"

"Sure. I have some at home. Come on over when you're finished."

The boys parted at the elevator in the lobby, and Frank and Joe went to the barbershop in the basement, where they had their hair dyed a reddish color. False eyebrows and cheek pads completed their disguise. Grinning contentedly, they took a taxi to Gummi's house.

"Boy, if I didn't know better, you could have fooled me," he said admiringly. "Here, put these on!" He handed them well-worn work clothes.

"Let's go down to the harbor and see if we can spot our friend Mar," Frank suggested when they had changed.

"Good idea. We can try our disguise on him," Joe said.

All three scrambled into Gummi's jeep. On the way, the Icelandic boy said, "One more thing. Don't speak English when those thugs are around!" He taught them a few Icelandic words, which, if muttered repetitively, would fool any foreigner.

They parked the car in the busy harbor area and strolled along the waterfront.

"Look!" Joe said said after a while. "Isn't that Rex Mar over there?"

"Right. He's checking out a trawler!" Frank exclaimed.

Mar was dickering with a sailor aboard a small fishing boat. Then he turned, smiled, and stepped back onto the dock.

"Let's go!" Frank said, and they walked directly toward the approaching seaman. Mar showed no sign of recognition. When they passed him, Frank deliberately stumbled into him. The man teetered back. Frank mumbled a few Icelandic words, and the boys walked on.

Out of earshot, Joe let out a muted whoop. "We did it, Frank! That old salt didn't recognize us at all!"

The boys turned to see Mar sizing up the trawler. She was about thirty-five feet long, broad of beam, with a squat, sturdy look. As the old fellow turned to go, the boys accosted him.

Mar's eyebrows nearly raised to the peak of his cap as Frank revealed their identity. Then Gummi was introduced. They shook hands.

"We saw you make a deal," Frank said. "When do we set sail?"

"This afternoon, if you're ready."

"We are. Okay, Gummi?"

"Right."

"We will meet on board at five o'clock," Mar said, then hastened off to lay in supplies.

At five-thirty that afternoon the little boat named *Asdis* churned out of Reykjavik Harbor and along the coast in the direction of Snaefellsjokull. Once safely at sea, Frank and Joe removed their cheek pads and eyebrows and fell to helping skipper Mar with chores on the deck.

By eight o'clock a stiff wind kicked up white-caps on the sea, and the boat began to rock. On the bridge, Mar regaled Frank and Joe with stories of Iceland.

On the wall behind the wheel was the Icelandic coat of arms. It showed a shield, which Frank recognized as the insignia on Icelandic coins. Standing on the right side of the shield was a giant, holding a staff. On the left side was a bull. Over the top loomed a dragon and a huge bird.

"What does it mean?" Frank asked.

"There's a legend behind it," Mar said, and Gummi nodded. As the storm worsened, the Hardys were told the story of a bad Viking king named Haraldur Gormsson, who wanted to conquer Iceland.

"But he realized he must send a scout to look

the place over," the old seaman explained, "so he sent his lieutenant, who turned himself into a whale to swim around the island."

"Like a spy submarine," Joe said.

Leaning against the side of the cabin for balance, Gummi laughed. "There was plenty of magic in those times. Same as today."

"Do you expect us to believe that?" asked Frank.

Rex Mar made a face. "Believe what you want, but that whale was met on the east shore by a furious dragon, breathing poisoned fire. The dragon was also accompanied by giant worms and snakes, so the whale withdrew."

Gummi took up the yarn. "Next he went to the north shore. There he found a huge bird, like a falcon, whose wings touched the mountain on both sides of a fjord. With him were other birds, big and small."

"And they scared the whale?" asked Joe.

"What else?" Mar chuckled. "On the west side, the whale was met by a bull, who came snorting and charging into the seas."

"All alone?" Joe asked.

"Oh no," said Gummi. "With him were other guardians of the island—the trolls and the hidden people. Naturally he scrammed out of there!"

Rex Mar scratched his head at the colloquial English which he had not heard before.

"On the south shore," Gummi continued, "the

whale saw a giant with an iron staff in his hand. This guy was taller than a mountain, and with him were many other giants. Nothing was left on the shore now but sand, glaciers, and heavy seas. So the whale withdrew and reported what he had seen to King Gormsson."

"Did the king tackle Iceland after that?" Joe asked.

"Not on your life! Today these four creatures are known as the defenders of Iceland."

The sea had become so rough by now that the skipper suggested everyone go below. He throttled back the engine and headed into the wind. But suddenly the gale shifted and the *Asdis* rocked violently.

Mar's face was impassive and showed no sign of fear, but Gummi was worried. "I've never seen a storm like this before," he said. He had barely finished speaking when the *Asdis* pitched forward. The entire crew was thrown to the deck!

CHAPTER XV

A Bad Break

WAVES crashed over the deck, nearly swamping the *Asdis*. The boys battened down the hatches while Rex Mar switched on the pump motor.

"I could do with some of Chet's seasick pills now!" Frank shouted above the howling gale.

The little trawler endured the buffeting by the elements for two hours before the storm let up a bit. Then the winds tapered off gradually, giving the crew time for catnaps before dawn lighted up the jagged coastline.

After a breakfast of cold lamb, bread, and milk, the boys joined Rex Mar at the wheel. "We'll spell you for a while, sir," Frank said. "You need some rest."

The Icelander accepted the offer, but would not go below. Instead, he stretched out on a bench and fell fast asleep.

While Frank held the wheel, Gummi read the

chart spread out on a table. "X marks the spot where we're to put ashore," he said.

Frank checked the coordinates. "Wow! Look here!" he called to Joe. "This is right near the place where we transferred to the *Albert!*"

The sturdy *Asdis* rode the waves for another hour, then Gummi awakened the skipper. "I think this is where we take her in," he said.

The old man stood up stiffly, looked at the map, then peered over the water at the sullen coastline. "*Ja.* There's the inlet."

Frank spun the wheel and guided the trawler toward shore. Near the mouth of the stony inlet, Joe exclaimed, "Hey, Frank! A rubber raft!" He reached for the binoculars on a shelf and whipped them to his eyes. "And it has a small outboard!"

"I didn't see a whale after all!" Frank said.

Joe moved toward the radio. "Shall I contact Captain Magnusson right now?"

"No. If Musselman is listening in on our wave length, it would give us away," Frank replied.

Mar made the *Asdis* fast to the makeshift dock in the inlet and said, "Now we will have to wait until the man contacts us."

"Meantime I'm going to check on that raft," Frank said.

While Gummi scrambled up a low ridge near the shore to keep a lookout, Frank and Joe climbed around the jagged shore to where the raft bobbed in a small rock-strewn inlet.

Joe was first to step into the craft. "It has a watertight canopy!" he exclaimed. "I've never seen one like this before. And look, Frank, these pontoons aren't metal. They're rubber, with valves like ballast tanks."

"You're right. See these little compressed air containers?"

Joe grew even more excited. "Of course! This is the underwater gimmick we suspected. Musselman was towed by the *Tek* until they came near this landing spot. Then he surfaced and beat it for shore!"

"At the same time we were transferring to the *Albert*. That was a close call for him!"

Frank and Joe left the raft as they had found it and returned to Gummi with their information.

"Those guys are no amateurs," the Icelandic boy said. "We'd better be careful."

They had to wait almost all day for their rendezvous. When dusk began to settle over the ocean, the skipper took his binoculars and scanned the shore. "Here comes our man now," he said, and handed the glasses to Frank. A jeep came bouncing over the rough ground. Musselman was at the wheel.

"In your disguises, quick!" Mar ordered.

Frank and Joe hastened below, attached their false eyebrows and padded out their cheeks. When they came on deck again, Musselman was there to greet them. Beneath his jacket bulged a pistol in a shoulder holster.

Frank chuckled inwardly at the confrontation. Disguise versus disguise! Obviously Musselman wore his to mislead Icelandic authorities, but the Hardys knew his secret. They hoped he would never discover theirs!

Now the man leaped nimbly on deck. Smooth-spoken, he complimented Mar for bringing the boat through such a fierce storm.

"You wanted a seaworthy boat, and I got one, Mr.——"

Musselman grinned. "Call me Chief, that's all you have to know." He glanced at the three boys, and his eyes returned to the skipper. "You will sail to Greenland for me, but we must avoid the Arctic Patrol."

"We are carrying contraband? What kind?"

A sly smile crossed Musselman's lips. "Are all Icelanders so inquisitive? Well, I'll tell you. I have three boxes of rare metal ore. A new find in this part of the world. But the Icelandic government will not let me take it out." He shrugged. "So we do it anyway. Bring your crew and follow me!"

The four leaped ashore and walked to the jeep with Musselman. It was an open-top vehicle, much like Gummi's. Mar sat in front, while the youths squeezed into the back.

The jeep banged and jounced over the rough

ground, heading for the interior. Presently a trail came in sight. It was nothing more than tire tracks which curved and undulated over the barren ground.

The driver increased his speed, and as they came to a bend around a small gully, the jeep slewed to the right and a rear wheel teetered over the edge.

"Look out!" Joe shouted.

The jeep banged on its rear axle before regaining the trail again. Musselman half turned his head toward the back seat.

"Did someone speak English?" he asked.

"*Nei*," Gummi replied.

"I have one bad ear," Musselman said. "I must have heard wrong."

Joe kicked himself mentally for the slip of the tongue and determined to be more careful in the future. One false move now, and all would be ruined!

Presently the ground became even rougher, and soon the jeep stopped. A hundred yards farther and halfway up the edge of a stony slope stood five ponies. The rugged little horses had shaggy coats and waited patiently as the five travelers approached.

The ponies were saddled and the party mounted. Musselman took the lead. They trudged along and rounded a bend in the valley, then turned into a

partially hidden glen, shielded by towering chunks
of lava.

Behind one of these stood a large sod hut built
into the hillside. A long thin antenna stuck out
of the roof.

Musselman stopped, and after they dismounted
led the quartet inside. The interior was sparsely
furnished, yet warm and comfortable. The table,
chairs, stove, and other accessories were modern.

The Hardys looked around for the three boxes.
None were in sight.

"Pretty elaborate setup, Joe," Frank murmured
to his brother out of Musselman's earshot.

Just then the door opened and another man
appeared. *Musselman's pal—the helicopter pilot who had lifted him off the glacier!* Now for the
first time they heard his name—Diran. He, too,
glanced at the Hardys without recognition, then
spoke in low tones with his accomplice.

After a meal of beans, bread, and cold meat,
Musselman dragged out some folding cots and
directed the boys to turn in for the night.

Then he and his confederate slipped out into
the darkness.

"Come on, Joe! Now is our chance!" Frank
said.

They hastily pulled on trousers and shoes, crept
across the earthen floor, pushed open the door
and went out into the night.

As they rounded a large lava boulder, they heard voices. Both boys ducked down. About ten feet ahead stood the two suspects. The men spoke in a language that neither one of the Hardys had ever heard before.

Suddenly a chill of fear struck them when Musselman mentioned the name "Hardy."

Was the boys' presence known? Had their cover been blown?

CHAPTER XVI

The Boxes

At hearing the name "Hardy," Frank's heart sank. No doubt the men were well armed. Making a break for it now would be foolhardy. The boys crept back into the sod house and whispered their discovery to Gummi and Mar.

"I wonder what they intend to do," Gummi said.

"Well, we have no choice but to play it by ear," Joe muttered glumly.

Only Musselman returned to the hut that night. His confederate remained outside. The boys concluded that he was guarding the door.

Shortly after daybreak Diran stepped in and began to prepare breakfast. He gave no sign of recognition and the boys were relieved. Perhaps everything was all right, after all.

Breakfast was a makeshift affair, with everyone

135

eating eggs and bread in tin plates wherever they could find a place to sit.

Sidling up to Rex Mar, Frank murmured, "Ask them about those boxes."

The seaman spoke in English. "The boxes with the contraband, Chief— I do not see any. Where are they?"

Musselman put down his plate and wiped his mouth with the back of his hand. "Not so fast, Mar. They are not here."

"Oh?"

With a crooked smile Musselman motioned to his accomplice. "Diran and I are leaving for a while. All of you stay here until we come back," he ordered. "More of my men are outside."

After they had left, Frank looked out the small window. Musselman and Diran disappeared behind a big volcanic boulder. "Come on," Frank said tersely to the others. "Let's search this place."

"Right," Joe added. "We might come up with a clue!"

The three boys, assisted by Rex Mar, left nothing untouched. They looked into every utensil, pounded the thin mattresses, and pulled out the cots to look beneath them.

Joe was about to replace Musselman's bed when his eyes caught a thin crack in the earth floor. "Hey, Frank, look at this!"

The boys dropped to their hands and knees.

Frank pulled out his pocketknife and worked it into the crack, which grew wider.

Following its course, the knifepoint outlined a square, between two and three feet wide.

"It's a trap door of some kind," Gummi declared.

Rex Mar stood by fascinated as the young detectives worked feverishly. Frank asked him to stand guard at the window in case the two thugs should return.

The boys prodded until they found a ring, which they pulled hard.

Up came the trap door!

A ladder led into the dark cellar. No light switch was in evidence. "Do you have a cigarette lighter, Mr. Mar?" Joe called out.

The man reached into his pocket and tossed a lighter. Joe flicked it on and descended.

"Holy crow, Frank! Come down and take a look at this!"

Frank climbed down the ladder, and the two found themselves standing in a small room, one side of which was literally covered with radio and electronic equipment.

"What a sending-and-receiving station!" Joe exclaimed.

Frank gasped as his eyes roved over the elaborate setup. "This is a top-quality spy center, Joe!"

The Hardys were skilled at radio transmission,

and knew how to operate much of the equipment which gleamed in the glow of the flickering lighter.

"Frank, I wonder what this is," Joe said, and lightly touched the edge of a highly polished metal box.

Suddenly there was a sizzing sound, accompanied by blue sparks. Without a word, Joe sank to the ground. The lighter fell from his hand and was extinguished.

An icy chill ran down Frank's spine as he stood in the pitch blackness. He dropped to his hands and knees and searched about until he found the lighter. *Flick*—it failed to respond. *Flick—flick.* Finally it burst into flame again, sending its feeble light over Joe's ashen face.

Frank felt for his brother's pulse. He was breathing. "I've got to get him out of here, and quick!" Frank thought.

Just then Gummi leaned over the trap door. "What's going on down there, fellows? Is everything all right?"

"No, Joe's been shocked," Frank replied. "Come on down and give me a hand. We've got to get him up."

Gummi descended, and together they lifted Joe's limp body from the floor. Gummi climbed the ladder first, tugging at the boy's arms. Frank stood beneath his brother, shoving as hard as he could. Soon the unconscious Joe was lying on the earth floor.

Frank rolled him quickly out of the way. Gummi replaced the trap door and patted the earth so that the cracks did not show. Then he put the cot back into place.

Frank, meanwhile, administered artificial respiration to his brother. Suddenly Rex Mar called out, "Here they come!"

"How far away?" Gummi asked.

"A hundred yards."

Frank worked like fury. Joe's eyes opened and Frank and Gummi pulled him to his feet. "Snap out of it, Joe!" Frank hissed, but his brother was still groggy.

Half dragging, half walking Joe to his cot, the boys put him down, tucked his hands in behind his head, and crossed his feet, making it look as if he were napping.

By now Joe was fully conscious but still weak and his left forefinger bore a slight burn.

"They stopped to talk," Mar reported.

Frank wondered what the discussion was about. The boxes, no doubt. A thought, half submerged in his subconscious, now came to the surface strong and clear.

Three boxes and three missing people!

Frank whispered his suspicion to Joe and Gummi. Joe looked sick with fear. Were Major McGeorge, Chet, and Biff "the rare metal ore" sealed in those boxes?

Gummi was more optimistic. "We haven't seen

the boxes yet," he said. "Maybe they're only small ones!"

Joe had a plan. He wanted to break out of the door just as the others were entering, grab one of the ponies, and race back to the *Asdis*. "I could radio for help," he said. "I'm certain these fellows have something to do with the missing astronaut."

"No doubt," Frank agreed, but cautioned against any rash move. "Gummi's right," he said. "We have to get a look at those boxes before we do anything."

"Quiet!" Mar ordered. "They are coming now."

The door opened and the two men stepped inside.

Gummi, who stood beside Frank, quickly stepped to the other end of the room. In doing so, his foot accidentally banged into Diran's leg. The fellow cursed and hit the Icelandic boy with the back of his hand. Gummi staggered before regaining his balance, but said nothing.

"Outside, all of you!" Musselman commanded. He spoke in English, and the Hardys pretended not to understand. The chief jerked his thumb toward the door. Frank and Joe walked out behind Gummi and Mar.

Waiting behind a boulder were three carts with ponies harnessed in readiness. The two men hopped into the first one and beckoned the others to follow. Mar got in one cart with Frank.

"That fellow Diran didn't curse in Icelandic," the seaman whispered.

"What was it?"

"Some kind of Balkan language. I heard it when I was shipping in the Black Sea."

The lead pony cart wound in and out among the boulders on a trail which slanted up the hillside. Finally the boys realized what their destination was when the yawning blackness of a cavern appeared before them.

Flashing powerful lights, Musselman and Diran drove right into the cave, beckoning the others to follow. Then Musselman stopped and everyone jumped down.

"Follow me!" ordered the chief.

They walked deeper until the light revealed three rectangular boxes in one corner of the volcanic cave. They were made of fresh wood and stood against the wall like oversized coffins!

CHAPTER XVII

Shut In

THE sight of the three boxes propped against the wall of the cave struck fear into the hearts of the boys. Joe gulped and looked about for a possible clue. His eyes lighted upon a khaki jacket crumpled on the hard floor. It bore the U.S. insignia of major!

No doubt any more. The astronaut must have been here! Frank also spied the jacket and glanced at Joe. Both had the same plan in mind. With Gummi and Mar they would make a break out of the cave at any cost, and try to get back to the *Asdis*.

Joe signaled Gummi, and Frank motioned to Rex Mar. Then Joe let out a bloodcurdling war whoop and made a dash toward the daylight at the mouth of the cave.

Frank and Gummi raced after him, but Mar had no chance to escape. Musselman had blocked his way the very instant Joe let out his cry.

Just as the three youths dashed into the open, the cave echoed to the crack of a pistol shot. Two men, lying in wait outside, reacted to the signal.

They jumped Frank and Gummi and sent them flying. Joe whirled around to join the fierce fracas which followed. Fists flew. Gummi was downed by a blow to the head, but Frank staggered his opponent with a right cross to the jaw.

Then Musselman and Diran plunged into the fray. A swinging pistol butt sent Joe Hardy to the ground. Frank was seized, and it was all over.

Pulling stout cords from their pockets, the men tied the boys' hands behind their backs.

Just then Rex Mar, looking bewildered, walked out of the cave. "What are you doing to my crew?" he demanded.

"Quiet!" Musselman snapped.

The three were dragged to their feet, still reeling under the impact of the assault.

"These boxes will be of good use after all," Musselman said and nodded toward the cave. Then he laughed loudly.

"The major and that fat kid would have been awful heavy anyway," one of his henchmen said.

"So would his buddy, the tall one," said the other.

Musselman looked grim. "That is not the point. Bring the boxes out. We will go back to the hut and await instructions."

The two fellows went inside and carried the

boxes out one by one. Then they stacked them on one cart. Musselman ordered the three boys into the second cart, which he drove himself, while Diran and Mar took the third.

Soon they were back at the sod hut. Frank, Joe, and Gummi were pushed inside and shoved onto the cots. Mar followed and fell into a chair.

Musselman and Diran sat down also, while the other two men lifted the trap door and disappeared into the radio room below.

"So we have captured the Hardy boys at last!" Musselman sneered.

"How did you recognize us?" Frank demanded.

"Your brother spoke English in a moment of danger. It was not very smart!"

Joe gritted his teeth. You won't get away with this, Musselman!"

His captor merely smiled and went on quietly, "We have gotten away with it already. And it was not easy. You slipped through our net in Bayport, but we caught the little sardines in Iceland!"

"Let us go!" Gummi hissed. "I'm an Icelander. My countrymen will find us and you'll pay for it, you finky foreigners!"

Color rose to Musselman's face. He pointed to Diran. "Mr. Ionescu and I happen to have Icelandic passports."

"Fake ones, of course," Joe said sarcastically.

"Why did you try to get rid of us?" Frank asked.

"We knew your father was working on the astronaut case and suspected he sent you up here to help."

Frank stiffened. So the spies had known all along that his father was involved in the case. Would they try to capture him, too—or perhaps had done so already?

"Then you tried to pose as Rex Hallbjornsson to get the fifty thousand dollars," Frank went on.

Their captor snapped his fingers. "Fifty thousand dollars! It is nothing compared to our real prize. We wanted you—as a ransom to get your father off the case, but now it is too late. You are expendable."

Diran Ionescu pointed a finger at his superior. "But you almost did not catch them. They slipped away at the airport, and they got off the glacier, too!" He laughed.

Musselman snarled, "Quiet! If you had had that plane's engines tuned up, I could have flown them to the east coast and then to our—"

He was interrupted by one of his henchmen, who poked his head through the trap door. "I just made contact. Plan B is in operation. They are on their way."

Musselman smiled. "Excellent. We are ready."

"Ready for what?" Frank thought frantically. He tried to stall further action by taunting their enemies. In a sarcastic voice he said, "You think you're clever. But we know you got Major Mc-George and threatened to throw him into the sulfur pit unless he gave you NASA secrets. And the Icelandic authorities know it, too!"

Musselman looked startled, and Frank went on, "But he wouldn't talk, would he?"

"He'll talk when we get him out of this country," Ionescu boasted. "Then we will have the facilities to make him talk!"

"And what is your Plan B?" Gummi spoke up.

Musselman shook his head and said, "You will never know."

Just then the sounds of a radio broadcast issued from the trap door. It was from the American base in Keflavik. In terse, short sentences the newscaster broke the big story:

"Major McGeorge has vanished on his trip to Iceland. A force of Marines is prepared to comb every nook and cranny of the island. . . ."

"Shut it off!" Musselman screamed and went below. The boys heard him send a message. When he reappeared, he said, "Into the boxes with them!"

The three boys were led outside. Despite the pleading of Rex Mar, they were roughly tossed into the boxes. They struggled, but it was of no use. The criminals shut the lids and secured the latches. Frank, Joe, and Gummi were sealed inside to meet their fate!

Mar was forced to help move the boxes onto

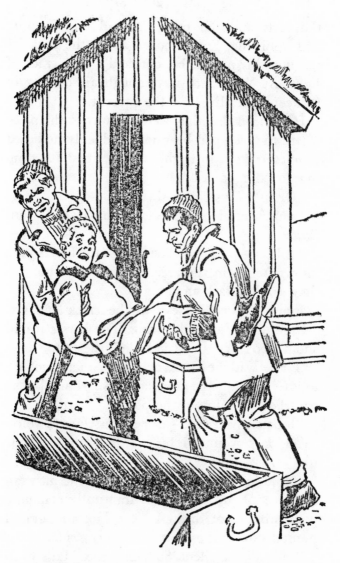

The boys were roughly tossed into the boxes

the carts and the ponies started off. Joggling and bouncing, Frank looked about the dark interior of his prison. He detected a thin crack of light. At least there was enough air coming in to keep him alive, for the present.

He judged that they were halfway to the place where the jeep had been left. Suddenly he heard Ionescu cry out in fright. "There it is! It's coming for the ponies!"

"Or us!" Musselman shrieked.

Frank heard Rex Mar shout the Icelandic word *isbjorn.*

Ice bear—polar bear! Several of the beasts were known to be in the area. If they were hungry, they would attack anything!

Frank pressed his eye to the crack and saw a large white form advancing. The horses reared and his box was almost jerked off the cart.

There was the crack of a rifle, then another, followed by a fierce growl and a snarl amidst the panicked neighing of the ponies.

"Ionescu, you fool!" came Musselman's voice. "You only wounded him. Run—run for your life!"

Rapid footsteps could be heard as the men ran for cover. Frank hoped his frantically galloping pony would not throw off the box and braced himself during the short but violent ride.

Then all was silent. Suddenly Rex Mar's voice

sounded above Frank's box. "The bear is after them!" he said hoarsely and opened the lid.

Frank jumped out and helped the seaman free Joe and Gummi.

"Why didn't you run away?" he asked Mar.

"The bear jumped over me and knocked me down. When I came to, they had already fled, and the beast was after them."

"If they escape the bear, they'll come back for us," Joe said. "We'd better scram."

"But then we'll never catch those spies!" Frank said. "I say we fill the boxes with rock. Would you be willing to stay and pretend we're still in there, Mr. Mar? Meanwhile, we'll make a run for the trawler and radio for help."

Mar nodded grimly. "They will not get away with this. I will stay!"

Quickly they collected chunks of lava, wrapped them in their jackets and put them into the boxes. Then they shut the lids. The men were still out of sight.

One had dropped his gun. Mar picked it up. "Just in case the bear comes back," he muttered. Then he lay down on the ground about ten yards away from the carts. "I will pretend to be unconscious," he declared. "This way they will not be suspicious. Now run and radio for help, quick!"

CHAPTER XVIII

Divide and Conquer!

THE trio set off at a fast trot. If they could reach the *Asdis* before Musselman and his gang, they had an outside chance of trapping the spies.

Frank took the lead for a while. The three ran, Indian file, dodging in and out behind the grotesque volcanic formations. Then Gummi took the lead until they came in sight of the jeep.

"Now we can ride the rest of the way," Gummi panted jubilantly. He sprinted and leaped into the driver's seat. But before he could start the motor, Frank ran up to him. "No, Gummi, that won't do!"

"Why not?"

"If the jeep's gone, they'll know someone took it."

"Frank's right," Joe stated. "We don't want to alert them."

"But when they reach the jeep, they'll overtake us," Gummi protested.

"I think not," Frank replied. "Don't forget they're carrying those three big boxes, and they wouldn't fit on the jeep, along with four men!"

Gummi reluctantly admitted that the Hardys were right. He hopped out of the vehicle and lifted the hood.

"What are you going to do?" asked Joe.

"Disconnect one spark plug. That ought to give them a little more trouble."

Then the three set out again. The short rest had relieved their aching muscles, and the smooth rhythm of their bodies carried them swiftly toward the shore.

Finally they came to the crest of a small rise, and halted to gaze down at the sea, churning and foaming on the rocks below. There, at the crude dock, bobbed the *Asdis*.

"What a welcome sight!" Frank called out.

The boys raced down the hill and onto the trawler. Joe's first reaction was to radio the Icelandic coast guard for help, but Frank opposed the move.

"If Musselman's crew has a radio, they might intercept our call."

"Then they'd have to change their plans again," Gummi said, adding, "That would be the end of poor Rex Mar."

"Then ambush is our only choice," Joe declared.

Frank grinned. "Divide and conquer!"

"How will we work it?"

"Let's talk about it over some chow, I'm starved," Frank suggested.

The boys quickly refreshed themselves with food and water, all the while discussing the best way to seize the enemy. By the time they had finished their snack, a basic plan had been worked out.

Frank was to hide in the lifeboat, which swung gently on its davits. Joe would secrete himself in a locker on the bridge, while Gummi would hide in the captain's quarters.

"It's going to be mighty rough," Frank said. "We'll have to take them one at a time."

"Suppose one of us gets into trouble—more than he can handle?" Gummi asked.

"Then we'll give a rebel yell," Joe suggested.

"It'll be all for one," Frank said. "Let's each get some rope so we can tie up our friends."

They found rope in a locker, then gathered on the bridge. Gummi took the binoculars and scanned the forbidding coastline.

"What if they don't come?" he asked nervously.

"Don't worry," Frank replied. "This caper is too big for them to drop it now."

"So we catch them. Then what?"

"We'll go back and search the cave. I have a hunch that someone is still there."

"Like who?" Gummi put the question without removing the glasses from his eyes.

"It could be that—"

"Here they come!" Gummi interrupted.

On the brow of the hill appeared a strange-looking caravan. In the lead was the jeep, occupied by four men. Tied to the back of the jeep were the pony carts. Two boxes were laid across one of them, the remaining box was in the second cart, along with Rex Mar.

"Okay, fellows, to your places!" Frank said.

Joe remained on the bridge. He opened a vertical locker, which contained only the captain's coat, squeezed in, and closed the metal door until only a crack remained.

Gummi hastened to the captain's quarters, where he hid behind the washroom door. Then Frank, making sure to keep himself shielded from view, lifted one end of the lifeboat cover.

He crept inside and peered out from beneath the canvas. Musselman's caravan jounced along.

"We've got them fooled so far," Frank thought as he watched Diran Ionescu brake the jeep to a halt by the dock.

Musselman turned to address the boxes behind him. "Here we are! Ready for the big ride?" He laughed and turned to his lieutenant. "They are not talking!"

"I suppose they know when they are defeated," Ionescu said. "All right, men, onto the boat with them!"

The three boxes were lugged onto the deck

and placed alongside the rail. Then Musselman ordered his crew to cast off. The engine was started and a low throbbing vibrated through the *Asdis*.

"Onto the bridge, Mar!" Musselman commanded.

"What do you want me to do?" Mar protested as Musselman shoved him roughly toward the wheel house.

"Head for Greenland! Once we are past the twelve-mile limit, over go the boxes."

"You are going to kill them?" Mar asked as he steered the boat out of the little cove.

Taking in every word, Joe Hardy shuddered at the thought of the fate that might have overtaken them.

"But what about me?" The old seaman sounded frightened.

"We will take care of you when we get to Greenland."

The spy stepped backward. Should Joe attack now? He could fling open the door hard, but before he could act, Musselman quickly left the bridge.

Joe opened the door wider. *"Psst! Captain Mar!"*

The skipper whirled around in astonishment, then an expression of relief came over his face.

Joe put a finger to his lips. Quickly he told where the other boys were stationed and added,

"The next guy who comes onto the bridge will get it!"

Mar nodded and smiled.

Frank, meanwhile, peered out from beneath the lifeboat cover. One of the two henchmen walked casually past and leaned on the rail to look over the sea. Silently Frank crept out of his hiding place. The davit rocked and squeaked, causing the thug to turn around. But Frank had already launched himself. He collided with the man in midair and together they sprawled on the deck.

The thug wore a look of complete amazement as he scrambled to his feet. Frank got in the first blow, a crushing right hand to the solar plexus!

"*Umph!*" His opponent doubled up, just as Frank delivered a stiff left to his chin. The man went down like a sack!

Quickly Frank bound his hands and feet. Then, struggling with all his might, he lifted him up and dropped him into the lifeboat. One down, three to go!

The boy stalked the deck, then ducked behind a stanchion as the second henchman came by. Swiftly Frank put his foot forward. The man tripped, landed on the deck, and turned, wild-eyed.

Frank grappled with him, but the wiry henchman wriggled from his grasp and ran along the deck, shouting, "They're out! Musselman, they're out!"

Instantly the chief and his lieutenant appeared. Musselman reached for his gun, but Frank bulled into him, head lowered. At the same time, he let out a bloodcurdling rebel yell.

Hearing, it, Joe dashed out of the locker and down the deck. Gummi came out of hiding and raced up the deck. The melee that followed was a bone-crushing battle. Each of the boys took an opponent.

Frank struggled to subdue Musselman, while his brother exchanged blows with Ionescu. Gummi had his hands full with the third man. They rolled over on the deck, scrambled up, and fought along the rail.

Suddenly Gummi was seized by the shirt front and lifted halfway over the rail. Another few inches and he would be cast into the cold sea!

Just then Rex Mar raced over and grasped the thug around the throat with his huge paw of a hand. Together, he and Gummi tossed the man over the rail. With a splash he hit the water and screamed for help.

Gummi grabbed a life jacket and threw it to him. The fellow clung to it, then disappeared far behind the boat in the wake.

Joe, meanwhile, was near exhaustion, battling the powerful Ionescu. Gummi came to his aid, distracting the spy for a split second. It took Joe only a moment to deliver a chop to the forehead. Ionescu went down.

Now Mar and the boys turned their full attention to Frank's fight. But Frank needed no help. He had Musselman on the rail, flailing him with rights and lefts.

The man's knees sagged and Rex Mar rushed over to seize him. He lifted Musselman overhead like a sack of grain, and threatened to drop him into the sea. Musselman screamed for mercy and Mar dropped him to the deck.

"So you were going to murder these boys!" he shouted. "Frank, Joe—tie him up. The captain is in command of his boat again!"

Mar went back to the bridge and radioed the coast guard for help. Then he turned the boat around. A few minutes later they picked up the man bobbing in his life jacket.

With all the criminals safely tied, Mar headed for the old dock. When he pulled up, Frank and Joe jumped ashore.

"Captain Mar, will you and Gummi wait here for us?" Frank asked. "We'll go back to the cave and search the place thoroughly."

"We sure will," Gummi replied, grinning. "The coast guard should be here shortly to take care of these jerks!"

"We should put *them* into the boxes and drop them in the ocean," Mar growled.

"We'd better leave their punishment up to the authorities," Joe said. "Well, keep your fingers crossed that we find Major McGeorge and the fellows!"

The boys waved, disengaged the pony carts, and set off in the jeep. Soon they reached the place where the ponies had been left. Each mounted one of the rugged little horses and rode to the sod hut.

Reaching it, they cautiously looked about in case any of Musselman's men were around. There were none. Joe found a flashlight in the hut, then they hastened to the cave. Inside, it was dark and gloomy.

"This is much bigger than I thought," Frank murmured as they made their way cautiously into the farthest recess. At the end, their beam illuminated a figure, bound and gagged, lying face down.

"Major McGeorge! Is that you?" Frank cried out as he raced ahead and bent over the man. There was no reply. "Here, let's roll him over, Joe!"

They grabbed the shoulder of the husky figure and rolled him face up. Their light shone upon a pale face with eyes closed.

It was Biff Hooper!

CHAPTER XIX

Hijackers!

WORKING speedily, Frank and Joe untied Biff, then carried him out of the cave into the daylight.

"He's in bad shape," Joe said worriedly as he glanced at the peaked countenance of their once-rugged friend.

"Come on. We'll give him a good massage," Frank suggested.

After the Hardys had stimulated Biff Hooper's circulation, their pal opened his eyes. He tried feebly to rise, but fell back onto the ground.

"Easy now," Frank said. "You're very weak, Biff. Where are Chet and Major McGeorge?"

With a blank expression, Biff looked straight ahead, as if not seeing the Hardys at all. Joe patted his face vigorously.

"Biff! Wake up! Tell us what's been going on!"

Biff's lips moved wordlessly. Finally, with great

physical effort, he whispered, "Bomb—bomb set to—"

"Good night, Joe! Let's get out of here before the cave blows up!"

Frank and Joe lifted Biff upright, with an arm over each shoulder and ran as quickly as possible.

Well away from the cave entrance, the boys stopped and glanced back. They had reached their ponies, but needed another one to carry the injured Biff.

"Look, Joe," Frank said, pointing to the side of the cave, "there's another pony grazing." The boys called to the animal, but it paid no attention to them.

"I'll go get him, Frank!"

"No! The whole place might blow up in your face! We'd better wait until—"

But Joe had already dashed toward the pony. If this had been the running track at Bayport High, he thought grimly, he would have set a new record for the 440!

He reached the pony, grabbed its tether, and pulled. The little horse responded instantly, running by Joe's side as he hastened with eyes half shut, anticipating the bomb explosion.

Perspiration streaming down his face, he returned to the others. Frank had helped Biff onto one of the ponies, but he leaned forward groggily over the animal's neck.

"We'd better tie him on," Joe panted as he pulled some rope from his pocket. Frank helped him, then they mounted their own ponies and rode on either side of Biff.

They set off at a brisk pace, but their backs were turned to the cave no more than a minute when a terrific *boom* shook the ground.

The concussion nearly knocked the three boys off their ponies, and Frank and Joe struggled hard to keep Biff upright. The animals reared in fear, but finally the Hardys regained control.

Joe glanced back over his shoulder to see a gaping, smoking hole where the small knoll once had been. "I hope Biff can explain everything," he thought as they plodded on.

Once they were in the jeep, their task was easier. Joe, at the wheel, gave it the gun, while Frank clung to Biff to keep him from bouncing out.

Joe handled the wheel like a race driver, cutting in and around the volcanic boulders. Finally he came to the rise of ground which overlooked the sea.

There, below them, lay two boats! The *Asdis* had been joined by the coast guard ship *Thor*. There was much activity on both decks. By the time the jeep reached the dock, Captain Magnusson and his men were there to meet the arrivals.

"We got Biff Hooper!" Frank called out. "He can't talk. Here, give me a hand with him!"

Crewmen from the *Thor* raced for a stretcher and carried Biff below deck where a first-aider worked to revive him. The skipper, meanwhile, lauded the Hardys for their catch.

"The president of Iceland should give you a medal for this!" he said, pumping their hands. "That Musselman's a bad one. Gummi told us how you bagged all four of them!"

Captain Magnusson had just finished telling the boys that the prisoners were now secured in chains on the *Thor,* when a helicopter appeared out of the blue. Moments later it landed neatly on the *Thor*'s afterdeck. The door opened, and out stepped Mr. Hardy.

"Dad!" Joe cried out as the boys ran to greet their father.

"Am I glad to see you two alive!" the famous detective said. "You were playing with dynamite. Musselman is known to be a ruthless international spy!"

"Dynamite is right," Joe said. "He nearly blew the three of us to kingdom come!"

The helicopter pilot, who had stayed with his craft, waved good-by and the chopper slid into the brisk air.

After introductions had been made all around, Captain Magnusson led the Hardys and their friends to his quarters. Everyone sat down, and conversation crackled with vital news.

Mr. Hardy's quest in Texas had turned up a

clue which had led to the unmasking of one of Musselman's cohorts.

"This man actually had an important job with the National Aeronautics and Space Administration," the detective reported. Interrogation had led to information that Frank and Joe were in grave danger.

"I hurried here as quickly as possible," Mr. Hardy continued, then added with a grin of satisfaction, "But you fellows got the job done before I arrived."

"It isn't finished yet, Dad," Frank spoke up. "And Biff may have the key to the riddle, if we could only get him to talk."

Just then the *Thor*'s first lieutenant came in with the news that the American boy was regaining full consciousness.

Frank and Joe went to Biff's room and found him greatly improved. But he still seemed unable to give a coherent story.

Captain Magnusson, who had followed the boys, suggested they let Biff rest for a while and have dinner. Soon everyone was seated around the large table, enjoying a hearty meal. Everyone but Rex Mar—who had been assigned three of the *Thor*'s men to bring in the *Asdis*.

After supper, Mr. Hardy grilled the four prisoners. They refused to answer even the simplest questions. Meanwhile Frank, Joe, and Gummi sat at Biff's side, trying hard to stimulate his memory. It was well after midnight when Biff cried out, "Frank, Joe, I think I've got it now!"

The boys, who had fallen asleep on makeshift bunks near their friend, jumped up excitedly and Frank ran for his father. Then everyone crowded around Biff.

"How about starting at the beginning," Mr. Hardy suggested.

Frank put in, "Gummi told us you got a message to meet us somewhere."

"Right," Biff began. "We received a telegram from Akureyri, saying you needed help and instructing us to take a private plane from Reykjavik which would be waiting for us."

"We thought you'd gone by boat!" Joe interrupted. "Chet mentioned something to Gummi about seasick pills!"

"Well, Chet had eaten a lot for lunch that day and his stomach was upset, so he bought some for the plane trip."

Joe grinned ruefully. "That's what you call a *mis*-clue!"

"On the plane," Biff continued, "we were socked and tied up. It landed on a small strip near the cave. Obviously they wanted us out of the way, so Frank and Joe'd be easier to handle."

"Then what happened?" Gummi inquired.

"We were supposed to be shipped to Greenland in three big boxes, together with Major

McGeorge. In case they had difficulties, there was an alternate solution which they called Plan B."

Frank and Joe exchanged excited glances.

"What was that?" Frank asked.

"McGeorge was to fly out together with Chet," Biff went on. "The astronaut and I are about the same size, and even look somewhat alike. He would travel under my name."

"Is that what finally happened?" Joe asked, his nerves on edge.

"I guess so. They took McGeorge and Chet away, and planted a bomb to blow up the cave. Musselman wanted to do it right away, but the guy he called Diran has a sadistic streak in him. He was going to give me a little more time!"

Frank clenched his fists when he heard of the devilish scheme of their enemies. "That animal!"

"Well," Biff concluded, "it didn't really make much difference to me. They hadn't given me any food or water, so I was in no shape to worry about anything."

"How were McGeorge and Chet to fly to Greenland?" Mr. Hardy wanted to know.

"I have no idea. I told you everything."

Everyone went back to sleep again until Captain Magnusson called them for breakfast. They had hardly finished eating when the *Thor* pulled into Reykjavik Harbor. The Hardys thanked the captain and his crew, then hopped into a taxi and sped directly to the airport. Gummi took Biff to the hotel.

At the airfield the Americans hastened to passport control. Mr. Hardy talked to an official who confirmed that Chet Morton and Biff Hooper had already passed through the gate.

"But that wasn't Biff Hooper at all!" Joe blurted out.

"Who was it, then? A criminal?" the man asked, perplexed.

"Anything but," Mr. Hardy said. He quickly told about the spies' plan.

"We'll have to stop the plane!" the official declared. "I hope they have not taken off yet. I think the flight to Scotland is scheduled to leave at eight-thirty."

"Scotland?" Frank cried out. "Weren't they going to Greenland?"

"No," the man replied. He led the Hardys into his office. There he quickly relayed a message to the tower.

"Prevent plane to Scotland from taking off! Abort take-off. Urgent!"

Instantly the request was relayed to the plane. No reply!

The Hardys and the airport official ran out to the field. The jet stood at the end of a runway, ready to speed down the white line.

"Dad, we have to stop it!" Frank yelled. Just then an airport jeep drove past. Frank flagged it down. He looked at the official, who nodded and barked an order in Icelandic to the driver. The man jumped out. Frank and Joe instantly hopped in and raced down the runway.

As Frank sped toward the plane, the big aircraft moved forward, its engines thundering. Car and plane were on a collision course!

CHAPTER XX

Cool Hand Chet

FRANK realized that a crash was imminent. He swerved to the left just as the craft became airborne. It whizzed overhead, its hot jet blasts barely missing the speeding car.

The plane virtually stood on its tail, reaching for altitude as fast as possible.

Frank drove the jeep back toward the airport buildings. The official waved them in the direction of the tower. When the boys reached the airport's nerve center, they found Mr. Hardy listening to the radio report from the Scotland-bound plane.

"If anyone follows us," the voice said, "we will shoot the pilot!"

"Good night!" Frank said. "They mean business."

"But they will not get away with it!" the tower dispatcher stated angrily.

Mr. Hardy followed the plane with binoculars

until it was out of sight, then watched on radar as the blip continued in an easterly direction.

"Maybe they're going to Scotland after all!" Joe said.

"Not likely," his father replied. "The plane's veering north." After a 180-degree turn the craft headed west.

By this time, government officials had arrived in the tower, and a plan was evolved within a few minutes. Both the United States authorities in Keflavik and the Danish Air Force in Greenland were notified. Within minutes, a dozen planes were launched from both bases.

Frank spoke up. "We'd like to be in on the chase."

"There's not much you can do now," an American officer replied. He stood next to Frank and introduced himself as Colonel S. P. Smith of the U.S. Air Force. "But we'll need you in Narssarssuaq."

"Is that the place where they are going to land?" Joe asked.

"I'm sure they don't plan to land there, but we'll try to force them down. We have them covered with an umbrella of planes."

The colonel led the Hardys out of the tower and onto the field, where they boarded a speedy military jet.

"We should be in Greenland in about half an hour," he explained.

No sooner had the Hardys fastened their seat belts than they were thrust backward by the terrific take-off speed of the jet. It whistled into the air, banked sharply, and headed west. Now relaxed in their seats, the trio chatted with Colonel Smith.

"So far everything is going like clockwork," he said. "That plane is a fish in our net."

"But what if the hijackers should get desperate and wreck the plane?" Joe asked.

"We'll just have to play it by ear," the colonel replied.

Now a voice crackled over the plane's P.A. system. "They are closing in," their American pilot said.

He had hardly spoken when the pilot in the hijacked plane snarled, "Stay away from us! If you try to force us down, we will crash the plane!"

Presently another of the pursuing pilots reported that the airliner suddenly had gone into a steep dive.

Colonel Smith barked a brisk order. "Ease off, but keep them in sight!"

"They must be madmen!" Mr. Hardy said gravely. "The lives of all those people are in jeopardy."

As the colonel pondered over what action to take, another voice came suddenly from the passenger plane.

"This is Major McGeorge. Do you read me?"

Colonel Smith and Mr. Hardy exchanged suspicious glances, before the colonel took the microphone.

"Your tricks won't accomplish anything!"

"It's no trick. This is really McGeorge. Chet Morton and I have everything under control. We will see you at Narssarssuaq! Over and out!"

Excitement ran high in the Hardys' plane. Soon the mountains of Greenland came into view and shortly afterward their pilot circled over the airfield at Narssarssuaq. It touched down and taxied to one side of the field.

Before the pilot could turn off the engines, Frank and Joe saw the hijacked airliner. It flew around the field once, then came in for a landing.

Two military planes followed directly behind and escorted the jetliner to the loading area. The portable stairway was quickly rolled to the rear door, and excited passengers streamed down the steps.

After all had debarked, the three Hardys and Colonel Smith dashed up the stairs and into the plane.

Along the aisle stumbled two men, their hands tied behind their backs. One had a bruised swelling on his forehead. The other, with a puffed right eye, glared out the window.

Behind them strode Chet Morton. "Come on there, out! Both of you!" he ordered. But when he saw the Hardys, he asked anxiously, "Hey, fellows, did you find Biff?"

"Yes. He's fine," Frank called out.

The prisoners were hustled out of the plane and taken into custody by military police. Then the crew and Major McGeorge stepped off the jetliner.

Introductions were made, hands clasped, and backs slapped. Then Colonel Smith led the Hardys, Chet, and the astronaut into an airport office. Here the incredible story of Major McGeorge's kidnapping was pieced together.

"I'm sure glad the government put such able detectives on my tracks," the tall, handsome astronaut said, and thanked Mr. Hardy and the boys for saving his life.

"Well, the last step you did yourself," Frank said with a grin. "How'd you manage to take over the plane?"

"I was recovering from the drug they had given me," the major explained, "and signaled Chet that I was all right."

"Then I did *it*," Chet put in, blushing. "One of those jerks who boarded the plane with us was up front and kept a gun on the pilot. I gave the other one an elbow in the ribs and finished him off with a karate chop to the forehead. *Pow!* Like this!" Chet made a fast motion with his right hand, and the Hardys chuckled.

"Your hobby really paid off!" Frank patted his friend on the back.

"After that," McGeorge went on, "we used the fellow as a screen and marched him up to the cabin. The other guy was completely taken by surprise."

"And Major McGeorge took care of him real fast," Chet concluded.

"Well, thank goodness it's all over," Mr. Hardy said. "Now tell us, Major, how did they ever get hold of you in the first place?"

"I was seized at gunpoint by three men after I had separated from our group at the sulfur pit to inspect the area. They put me into a helicopter and flew me to a cave."

"That's not there any more," Joe told him. "They blew it up."

"I know. A time bomb was set when they took Chet and me out. Good thing you found Biff Hooper before it went off!" The major went on to say that he was interrogated for hours, but would not reveal any NASA secrets.

"Then they took me back to the sulfur pit and threatened to throw me in," he reported.

"That's where we picked up your trail," Frank spoke up.

"Well, those devils circled around the pit, and when I still would not talk, they drove me away again."

The Hardys learned that in the early confusion following the disappearance of the major, the helicopter had made a clean getaway.

"A chopper was found abandoned on the east coast," Mr. Hardy put in. "I'm sure it was the same craft."

Frank snapped his fingers. "East coast! I bet that's where we were headed when Musselman kidnapped us in his plane."

"Could be," Mr. Hardy replied. "They had a speedboat hidden in a cove. I think they planned to take you out and dump you in the Atlantic."

By midafternoon Major McGeorge, the Hardys, and Chet Morton had returned to Reykjavik. At the Foreign Office they learned that Musselman and Ionescu still were tight-lipped. One of their men, however, was telling all he knew about the spies to save himself from a life behind bars.

It was revealed that the thugs were spies for hire. A foreign power had set up the diabolic plan to kidnap an American astronaut, then take him to their country, claiming that he had defected.

"Iceland proved to be an effective place to carry out the kidnapping," Anders Sigurdsson told them. "Our country is entirely law-abiding and nobody would ever suspect such a thing could happen here."

"But how could such elaborate preparations have been made so far in advance?" Frank asked, recalling the sod hut with all its sophisticated equipment.

"The agents have been here for a long time," Mr. Sigurdsson explained. "They were spying on your military base and knew far ahead of time that the astronauts were scheduled to visit Iceland."

Biff Hooper, meanwhile, had recovered enough to have supper with his pals and Mr. Hardy in the Saga's beautiful rooftop restaurant. They looked down over the harbor, now blinking with light, and while dining on a delicious dish of hot smoked lamb, talked with their guest Major McGeorge.

In the middle of the meal, Captain Sigtryggsson of the coast guard entered with his niece Steina. They were escorted to the Hardys' table, where introductions were made.

After complimenting the astronaut and Chet on their escape, Captain Sigtryggsson said, "I'm so pleased to meet you, Mr. Hardy. Your sons and their friends have been of great service to Iceland."

As the waiter pulled up a chair for the two newcomers, the door opened again and in strode Rex Mar. He was neatly dressed in a dark suit and joined the Hardys' table.

The detective shook the old man's hand vigorously and thanked him for all he had done for the American boys.

"They have done something for me, too," Mar replied with a smile. "They made me rich!"

"What are you going to do now, Mr. Mar?" Joe asked. "Buy yourself a fishing trawler?"

"Sure," Frank added. "You can go into business—"

"With me, for instance," came a voice from the door. Everyone cheered as Gummi walked toward the table.

"Will you be my lieutenant?" Rex Mar asked him.

"Why not?"

They laughed and chatted about their adventure, little knowing that a new one, *Mystery of the Bombay Boomerang,* was soon to come their way.

Finally Frank rose and requested everyone to be silent.

"There's one more thing," he said. "We found something near the sulfur pit which we should return to its owner!" With that he pulled a black glove from his pocket and handed it to Major McGeorge.

The astronaut's eyes opened wide. "What detectives!" he exclaimed.

"Yow! Yow!" Chet agreed.

ORDER FORM

BOBBSEY TWINS™
ADVENTURE SERIES

by Laura Lee Hope

Now that you've met the Bobbsey Twins, we're sure you'll want to "accompany" them on their exciting adventures. So for your convenience, we've enclosed this handy order form.

49 TITLES AT YOUR BOOKSELLER
OR COMPLETE AND MAIL THIS
HANDY COUPON TO:

GROSSET & DUNLAP, INC.
P.O. Box 941, Madison Square Post Office, New York, N.Y. 10010

Please send me the Bobbsey Twins™ Adventure Book(s) checked below @ $3.95 each, plus 50¢ *per book* postage and handling. My check or money order for $_____ is enclosed.

☐ 1. Of Lakeport	8001-X	
☐ 2. Adventure in the Country	8002-8	
☐ 3. Secret at the Seashore	8003-6	
☐ 4. Mystery at School	8004-4	
☐ 5. At Snow Lodge	8005-2	
☐ 6. On A Houseboat	8006-0	
☐ 7. Mystery at Meadowbrook	8007-9	
☐ 8. Big Adventure at Home	8008-7	
☐ 9. Search in the Great City	8009-5	
☐ 10. On Blueberry Island	8010-9	
☐ 11. Mystery on the Deep Blue Sea	8011-7	
☐ 12. Adventure in Washington	8012-5	
☐ 13. Visit to the Great West	8013-3	
☐ 14. And the Cedar Camp Mystery	8014-1	
☐ 15. And the County Fair Mystery	8015-X	
☐ 16. Camping Out	8016-8	
☐ 17. Adventures With Baby May	8017-6	
☐ 18. And the Play House Secret	8018-4	
☐ 19. And the Four-Leaf Clover Mystery	8019-2	
☐ 20. The Mystery at Cherry Corners	8020-6	
☐ 24. Wonderful Winter Secret	8024-9	
☐ 25. And the Circus Surprise	8025-7	
☐ 27. Solve A Mystery	8027-3	
☐ 47. At Big Bear Pond	8047-8	

☐ 48. On A Bicycle Trip	8048-6	
☐ 49. Own Little Ferryboat	8049-4	
☐ 50. At Pilgrim Rock	8050-8	
☐ 51. Forest Adventure	8051-6	
☐ 52. At London Tower	8052-4	
☐ 53. In the Mystery Cave	8053-2	
☐ 54. In Volcano Land	8054-0	
☐ 55. And the Goldfish Mystery	8055-9	
☐ 56. And the Big River Mystery	8056-7	
☐ 57. The Greek Hat Mystery	8057-5	
☐ 58. Search for the Green Rooster	8058-3	
☐ 59. And Their Camel Adventure	8059-1	
☐ 60. Mystery of the King's Puppet	8060-5	
☐ 61. Secret of Candy Castle	8061-3	
☐ 62. And the Doodlebug Mystery	8062-1	
☐ 63. And the Talking Fox Mystery	8063-X	
☐ 64. The Red, White and Blue Mystery	8064-8	
☐ 65. Dr. Funnybone's Secret	8065-6	
☐ 66. The Tagalong Giraffe	8066-4	
☐ 67. And the Flying Clown	8067-2	
☐ 68. On The Sun-Moon Cruise	8068-0	
☐ 69. The Freedom Bell Mystery	8069-9	
☐ 70. And the Smoky Mountain Mystery	8070-2	
☐ 71. In a TV Mystery	8071-0	
☐ 72. The Coral Turtle Mystery	8072-9	

SHIP TO:
NAME _____
(please print)

ADDRESS _____

CITY _____ STATE _____ ZIP _____

Printed in U.S.A.   **Please do not send cash.**

ORDER FORM

HARDY BOYS
MYSTERY STORIES*

by Franklin W. Dixon

Now that you've met Frank and Joe Hardy, we're sure you'll want to read the thrilling books in the *Hardy Boys* ® adventure series.

To make it easy for you to own all the books in this exciting series, we've enclosed this handy order form.

59 TITLES AT YOUR BOOKSELLER OR
COMPLETE THIS HANDY COUPON AND MAIL TO:

GROSSET & DUNLAP, INC.
P.O. Box 941, Madison Square Post Office, New York, N.Y. 10010

Please send me the *Hardy Boys*® books checked below. My check or money order for $_____ is enclosed and includes 50¢ per book postage and handling. (Please *do not* send cash.)

The Hardy Boys Mystery Stories® @ $3.95 each:

☐	1.	Tower Treasure	8901-7	☐ 30.	Wailing Siren Mystery	8930-0
☐	2.	House on the Cliff	8902-5	☐ 31.	Secret of Wildcat Swamp	8931-9
☐	3.	Secret of the Old Mill	8903-3	☐ 32.	Crisscross Shadow	8932-7
☐	4.	Missing Chums	8904-1	☐ 33.	The Yellow Feather Mystery	8933-5
☐	5.	Hunting for Hidden Gold	8905-X	☐ 34.	The Hooded Hawk Mystery	8934-3
☐	6.	Shore Road Mystery	8906-8	☐ 35.	The Clue in the Embers	8935-1
☐	7.	Secret of the Caves	8907-8	☐ 36.	The Secrets of Pirates Hill	8936-X
☐	8.	Mystery of Cabin Island	8908-4	☐ 37.	Ghost at Skeleton Rock	8937-8
☐	9.	Great Airport Mystery	8909-2	☐ 38.	Mystery at Devil's Paw	8938-6
☐	10.	What Happened At Midnight	8910-6	☐ 39.	Mystery of the Chinese Junk	8939-4
☐	11.	While the Clock Ticked	8911-4	☐ 40.	Mystery of the Desert Giant	8940-8
☐	12.	Footprints Under the Window	8912-2	☐ 41.	Clue of the Screeching Owl	8941-6
☐	13.	Mark on the Door	8913-0	☐ 42.	Viking Symbol Mystery	8942-4
☐	14.	Hidden Harbor Mystery	8914-9	☐ 43.	Mystery of the Aztec Warrior	8943-2
☐	15.	Sinister Sign Post	8915-7	☐ 44.	Haunted Fort	8944-0
☐	16.	A Figure in Hiding	8916-6	☐ 45.	Mystery of the Spiral Bridge	8945-9
☐	17.	Secret Warning	8917-3	☐ 46.	Secret Agent on Flight 101	8946-7
☐	18.	Twisted Claw	8918-1	☐ 47.	Mystery of the Whale Tattoo	8947-5
☐	19.	Disappearing Floor	8919-X	☐ 48.	The Arctic Patrol Mystery	8948-3
☐	20.	Mystery of the Flying Express	8920-3	☐ 49.	The Bombay Boomerang	8949-1
☐	21.	The Clue of the Broken Blade	8921-1	☐ 50.	Danger on Vampire Trail	8950-5
☐	22.	The Flickering Torch Mystery	8922-X	☐ 51.	The Masked Monkey	8951-3
☐	23.	Melted Coins	8923-3	☐ 52.	The Shattered Helmet	8952-3
☐	24.	Short-Wave Mystery	8924-6	☐ 53.	The Clue of the Hissing Serpent	8953-X
☐	25.	Secret Panel	8925-4	☐ 54.	The Mysterious Caravan	8954-8
☐	26.	The Phantom Freighter	8926-2	☐ 55.	The Witchmaster's Key	8955-6
☐	27.	Secret of Skull Mountain	8927-0	☐ 56.	The Jungle Pyramid	8956-4
☐	28.	The Sign of the Crooked Arrow	8928-9	☐ 57.	The Firebird Rocket	8957-2
☐	29.	The Secret of the Lost Tunnel	8929-7	☐ 58.	The Sting of The Scorpion	8958-0

SHIP TO:

NAME

(please print)

ADDRESS

CITY   **STATE**   **ZIP**

Printed In U.S.A.   **Please do not send cash.**